THE RIVER OF SOULS

Story by Mark Piggott
Poetry by Ashley Valitutto

Curious Corvid Publishing, Ohio

Curious Corvid
PUBLISHING

To my soulmate,

I would cross the heavens to be with you . . .

Our souls are like a river -
scenic and serene.
Sometimes, when the river rages,
the soul splits in two.
As the water crashes,
the spirit swirls around itself -
a rebirth, a reintroduction.
How lucky are we that this soul
landed in you and I?
How lucky are we to dance in each other's arms
and to know the warmth of one another?
To speak our own language.
To be a basin full of sweet wine
that only we know the taste of.
To be an echo in eternity
that only we know the sound of.
When the river flow stops,
sending us into separate spiritual realms,
I know you will find me.
I know you will seek me out.
I know you will answer my call from wherever you are,
and with your last breath,
fight to breathe new life into me.

He laid on the ground, disoriented beneath the weight of the wreckage pinning him to the road. He felt no pain, most likely because his spine was severed. The car had come out of nowhere, spinning out of control as it flipped through the air and slammed into him. The rain pelted his face. He drank in the droplets like sweet wine. It was the only comfort he had as he lay there dying.

Typically, this was where your life would flash before your eyes, but that didn't happen here. He had never really had much of a life . . . He worked a steady job with little to no social life. No family or friends to speak of either. He had a lonely, sheltered existence, and no one would cry over his grave.

Please, God, I don't want to be left alone!

He heard a voice in the distance—a woman's voice—crying a solemn prayer. *Did the driver hit someone else? Is she injured or dying too?* he pondered. He was not able to turn his head to look for the woman. Instead, he could only hear her torment through the falling rain. It was torture to listen to her pleas go unanswered.

"I'm sorry, I'm so sorry," he muttered breathlessly as his life slipped away. "Please, God, I don't want to die like this! Let me help her, please! Let me make something of my life!"

Those were his last words as he died, alone on a quiet road—only to be reborn on a distant world.

"**P**lease, God, I don't want to be left alone!" Alyssa prayed.

The sky opened up and rain poured down from the heavens as if the world was crying uncontrollably. The drops were heavy, saturating the ground in their fury as the storm soaked everything with reckless abandon, Alyssa sat there on the ground, cradling him in her arms gently as she added her tears to the pouring rain. She could barely hold up his massive body against the downpour. With the added weight of her grief, it took everything she had to hang on to him.

She used her wings to shield them from the rain, but the tiny, leathery wings on her back could barely stay open in this storm, let alone protect her from the torrent. She wrapped her tail around the lower body of her companion to help support his weight as she cradled him lovingly. The rain exposed her twisted black horns as her wet hair flattened against her head. Alyssa was a Dragonkin, and the man she loved just died in her arms.

"Great Mother of the Dragons, help me save him," she screamed. "I will give anything to you if you just restore his life! If his soul is already beyond the veil, then send someone to fill that void, please! As long as he is kind and compassionate, I could learn to love him.

"Please, God of the Heavens, take what you want from me. Just don't leave me alone in this place!" She kissed his forehead as she continued her plea to a higher power to help in her time of need. His skin was already cold and lifeless. Alyssa had only one chance to save him, but she knew it was a gamble. "The spell of restoration—it has to work! Please God, please let this work!"

Alyssa placed her hand over his head, then his heart as she chanted the spell. She fumbled the words, forcing them out through her tears and pleas.

"*Reach thairis air nèamhan nèimh; na leig le bàs buaidh fhaighinn,*" she began. "*Fosgail an doras tro ghràs Dhè; nach e seo an t-àite-fois mu dheireadh aige!*"

Her spell translated, "Reach beyond heaven's veil; do not let death prevail. Instead, open the door through God's grace; let this not be his final resting place!"

It was a last resort spell for an Oracle of Delphis Kai to restore some semblance of life to an empty shell. As practitioners of the healing arts, the oracles tapped into the healing power of light. The magic reached across the heavens, through time and space, to find a soul willing to fill the void left behind.

Alyssa continued to pray to whomever was listening, but the body in her arms remained still and cold. She cried and rocked back and forth as the rain drenched her lithe frame. She never noticed the soft glow that descended into his body. Like a will o' the wisp, it burned with the light of a single soul as it touched the heart of her beloved.

With a single breath, he lived again . . . Alive in a new world, in a new body, to save a voice that cried out to him into the darkness.

He awoke in comfort, laying on a plush, down mattress, surrounded by crisp, soft sheets and a warm wool blanket. His head buzzed from the slight headache pulsing in his temples. He rubbed his eyes and then his forehead, trying to drive away the pain. He barely opened his eyes, but he could see the sun was just setting outside. Water droplets beaded on the glass window, sparkling like tiny diamonds through the sunlight.

He remembered the rain, the downpour that drenched him from head to toe, but beyond that, his memory was fuzzy. Instead, he recalled two sets of memories as if they were fighting for dominance in his mind. *Maybe that's where my headache is coming from.* He tried to sit up, but he barely had the strength to raise his head from the pillow.

"Please don't try to get up," a voice pleaded with him as a gentle hand forced him to stay in bed. He turned to see Alyssa sitting next to him. Although she spoke a strange language, he understood every word she said, but it took him a moment to focus and follow what she was saying.

Out of the pouring rain, it was clear to see the beauty sitting before him. At first, her appearance caught him off guard, but that notion quickly passed. Alyssa's shoulder-length red hair framed her beautiful face, even as her twisted dragon horns stretched back from her forehead. Her beauty was highlighted with full red lips and deep green eyes, showing her deep concern as she wrung out the damp cloth. Her wings were barely visible, folded neatly against her back. She wore a flowing white shirt under a leather corset that supported her ample bosom as a skirt covered her legs and hid her tail beneath the ruffles of a petticoat.

She took the cloth from a basin and placed it on his forehead. He felt an overwhelming sense of relief as he stared in awe at her beauty with piqued curiosity.

"I know you, don't I?" he prodded inquisitively.

His question caught her off guard, but she surmised that his near-death experience had affected his memory. "Of course you do. I'm Alyssa, your . . ." she paused before answering. She realized the shock of his rebirth might have affected his mind. If she told him something he was not ready to hear, it could take him longer to recover. "I'm your maidservant."

"Servant?" Her answer perplexed him even more. It did not seem right, but his head hurt so much that he decided not to pursue it right now. "What happened to me?"

"You've been very ill for the past month from exposure to Dragon Dust," she responded. "I've been taking care of you."

Dragon Dust was a lethal poison to humans. He rubbed his head even more, trying to push through the fog of memories that swirled around inside. "I don't remember anything," he exclaimed. "I can't even remember who I am or where I am."

"Your name is Malcolm Seger," Alyssa explained as she continued to dab his forehead. "We are in the parish of Fairhaven in the Kingdom of Fawleen."

All of that seemed familiar to Malcolm as if it stirred a memory.

"Fairhaven," he pondered aloud. "I came here to retire after the war, yes? The war between Fawleen and Drogon."

Fawleen and Drogon had fought what people called "The Endless War," as it went on for more than 300 years. The humans of Fawleen and the Dragonkin of Drogon clashed over borderlands, water rights, trade disputes, and the biased views of leaders on both sides of the conflict. Four generations fought and died in the war. That all changed when one sect of Drogon—the Oracles of Delphis Kai—joined Fawleen in opposition to their people and worked to end the war. The Oracles were healers and pacifists, the opposite of the Acolytes of Hecat Tei and their dark chaos magic that ruled Drogon. In the end, the Oracles' treason was the deciding factor that brought peace to the troubled land.

Alyssa smiled with joy. She was surprised that he remembered something so distinctly and so quickly after his rebirth. *Perhaps a part of him is still there.* In her heart, Alyssa hoped he would remember more. "Yes, we did. Do you remember anything else?"

He rubbed his eyes again, trying to force himself to recall something, anything, but his mind came up blank. "No, I'm sorry. It's all a fog right now."

Almost immediately, her heart sank, but Alyssa put on a brave smile to hide her pain. "Well, you were very sick, so give it time. I'm sure your memory will come back," she explained as she rose from her chair. "If you're up to it, I'll bring you something to eat and some tea."

Malcolm looked at her and could see she was hiding her emotions. There was more to their relationship than she was letting on, but he was tired and confused. So, for now, he would leave things as they were. "That would be great. Thank you, Alyssa."

She picked up the water basin and took it with her into the next room, closing the door behind her. Malcolm just laid there in bed. As he stared at the ceiling, he tried to gather his thoughts. He remembered his life as Malcolm Seger, but there was something else elusive and far-reaching in the back of his mind. He recalled an accident, a woman's voice crying in the night. Perhaps it was Alyssa he heard; her voice was familiar, yet he couldn't be sure. For now, he just needed to clear his mind. Then maybe, just maybe, he would remember.

The marmot stew that Alyssa served him was delicious, and the tea warm and inviting. Afterward, as he lay in bed and started to doze, he heard it. Her voice was intoxicating as she sang while she washed up dishes in the kitchen. He listened to her sweet voice echo through the house as Alyssa sang her poetic melody, a simple song that lulled him to sleep. It was a lullaby, one that could hush a thousand crying children to a restful sleep. He felt all the pain, all the worries and trepidations wash away as he drifted off.

"Sleep now, my beloved one,
for your healing has just begun.
A dragon is here to guard you
while you rest to become anew.
I offer rebirth with my fiery breath
so you can rise again even after death.
My scales safeguard your body like a shield.
A form of defense that is hardened and steeled.
My wings wrap around your body like a cloak.
Feel the magic comfort you, precious folk.
A dragon is here to guard you
and help you see it through and through."

A rooster crowed, causing Malcolm to stir from his slumber. He shifted his body as he stretched his stiffened muscles. He slept well last night, better than he could remember. He wondered if the lullaby Alyssa had sung had some magic infused in it that helped him sleep so soundly. In any case, as he stirred under the covers, he felt utterly restless and needed to get out of bed.

Malcolm pulled back the sheet and blanket before swinging his legs over the side of the bed. The floor was cold to the touch as he wiggled his toes on the wood. He rolled his shoulders, giving his muscles much-needed exercise. It was then that Malcolm noticed the single gold ring on his left hand—a wedding ring. *But then who . . .* his thoughts turned to Alyssa. *What isn't she telling me, and why not?*

He shook his head, deciding he would ask her about it later. Malcolm braced himself on the bedpost as he got to his feet. He was a little unsteady at first, so he just stood there until everything settled. Then, he took a few steps, gingerly, over toward the dresser. Malcolm stared into the mirror hung over the bureau as he tried to recognize the face staring back at him.

Long black hair hung down to his shoulders, with gray streaks at the temples. His face was rather careworn, with a thick beard highlighted with gray on his chin and mustache. It showed age, but he wasn't old; simply experienced in love and war. Scars covered his upper torso, each one from a different battle. As he touched each of them, Malcolm tried desperately to remember where and how he got them.

The bullet hole in his left bicep was from a Drogon magi-gunner at an ambush at Clifden Falls. The sword slashes laid out across his chest that he received in the Borosh Highlands. He felt along the lower right side of his abdomen, looking for a scar that was not there. *Where's my appendix scar?* He pulled at his skin, but nothing was there.

A loud clang of dishes broke him out of his trance. He could hear Alyssa working in the kitchen, probably preparing breakfast for him. He scoured through the dresser drawers to find some pants and a shirt to wear. He took his time getting dressed, sitting on the edge of the bed so as not to fall and hurt himself while buttoning his shirt and pants.

Malcolm stood up, bracing himself as he walked over to the door. When he opened it, the smell of sausage, eggs, and toast filled his nostrils. The delicious smell made his mouth water. He slowly walked down the corridor, holding onto the walls with each step. He passed a small bathroom and another small room, like a study, on his way to the main room of the one-story house. It was a large room with a massive hearth and comfortable furniture on one side, with a kitchen and dining table across the room from it. He noticed a blanket and pillow on the sofa. *Is this where she's been sleeping all this time?*

Alyssa stood over the stove, cooking three things at once. But then, Malcolm noticed something he hadn't before - a glint of gold on her finger. As he looked at the ring on his hand, he knew the answer to his earlier question; but for now, he would have to wait and let Alyssa explain it to him.

"That smells delicious!" he said, startling her. She nearly dropped the frying pan when she heard his voice.

"Malcolm, what are you doing out of bed? You are in no condition to be moving about!" Alyssa scolded as she put the pan down and rushed over to his side.

"Sorry, but between my restlessness and the smell of your cooking, I couldn't help but get out of bed." Alyssa braced herself under one of his arms as she helped him over to a chair at the dining table.

"My cooking isn't worth you hurting yourself," she continued to admonish him. "You could have fallen, hit your head, or worse!"

"Well, I'm already up, so I might as well stay out here. Is that alright with you?"

Alyssa just sighed and shook her head as she gave in. She helped him over to the dining room table and sat him down in the chair. "Now, just sit there while I finish making us breakfast," she added before heading back over to the stove.

"Are you sure I can't help you? I could set the table or pour the coffee."

"No, thank you. Even if I let you, I would just have to follow right behind you and do it the right way."

Malcolm was hurt by her insult. "Really? Am I that useless?"

"No, you are far from useless. You have many admirable qualities, but cooking is not one of them," Alyssa began as she turned toward him, waving her spatula as she spoke. "Don't you remember the siege at Balflora? After we finally broke the enemy lines, you decided to cook everyone a celebratory feast. I had to treat half the squad for dysentery, and we all took an oath never to let you cook anything ever again."

Her humorous story stirred a specific memory within Malcolm, but he sensed something. Another memory, perhaps from another place, mixed with those of his life with Alyssa. It confused him, so he tried to stay focused on those involving his wife. "Yeah, I guess cooking a rhinoc vulture wasn't a good choice for a stew. They're awfully tough to chew, gamey too." Alyssa was glad to hear that his memories were slowly returning to him. "But I remember something else," he continued, "a restaurant, or maybe a diner. I was a cook there, I think. I . . . I can't recall!" Malcolm rubbed his eyes as his head pulsed in pain from the confusion.

Alyssa could see his frustration and decided to change the subject and keep him focused on the here and now. "Do you remember when we took that picture?" she motioned toward the fireplace. Malcolm turned his head and looked at the crowded mantelpiece. A sharpshooter's magi-rifle was mounted just above the mantel while neatly arranged medals, plaques, and memorabilia sat on the large wooden beam.

Centered on the mantelpiece, in a place of honor, was a single photograph. The photo, printed on metal, was clear as the day they had taken it.

It showed a group of seven soldiers wearing light armor under long leather coats, each one holding a magi-rifle like the one over the fireplace. Malcolm recognized himself in the photo, even some of the men and women standing there with him. He also recognized the only Dragonkin in the picture. Alyssa was there, standing right next to him, with one hand on his arm. They were standing in a place of honor, in the center, with everyone else gathered around them. It was a memorable day.

"Do you remember?" Alyssa asked again as she placed the plates of food down on the table. Malcolm looked over at her and smiled. Seeing that picture brought his memories into focus, and his headache slowly passed. He beamed as he thought of that particular day.

"Yes, I remember . . . We were both members of the 55th King's Musketeers, Zephyr Brigade. That picture was taken just before the Massacre at Chronost Pass when I asked you to marry me, and you said yes." His revelation startled her as it brought a smile to her face and a tear to her eye. "We couldn't officially get married, legally, so old Bertram performed a simple ceremony himself with the rest of the squad acting as witnesses. That was the last photo of all of us together. They were all killed in battle. You and I were the only survivors."

Alyssa's heart raced, overjoyed that his memories were returning. She knelt next to him and took his hand, kissing it lovingly, as she quietly thanked God. "Oh Malcolm, you do remember, you do!"

He reached down and lifted her chin so he could look into her eyes. "Yes, I remember, although my head is still fuzzy about certain things. Why did you feel the need to lie to me, say you were my maidservant?"

"I don't know," she started, laughing at the sheer insanity of her ploy. "With everything that happened, I wasn't sure if you would regain your memories or not. It was the first time I ever used the spell of restoration."

"Restoration? What exactly happened to me?"

Before Alyssa could answer him, they heard a noise outside. It was the sound of horses riding up to the house.

While Malcolm wondered who would be coming out at this time of the morning, Alyssa became frightened, as if she knew who it was.

"Stay here, please. Let me handle this!" Alyssa said as she jumped to her feet and rushed outside.

"Handle? Handle what?" Malcolm asked, but his request went unanswered as she slammed the door behind her. Immediately he could sense tension, but only muffled voices reached his ears. Disliking how the ensuing argument sounded, Malcolm forced himself to his feet. He struggled with each step over to the window, but his concern for Alyssa gave him an adrenaline rush. Once there, he stood just out of sight, peering between the parted curtains.

Alyssa stood on the front porch, just above the top step. She clenched a piece of paper in her hand, showing it to the two men in front of her. They stood on the ground before her while two others hung back by the horse-drawn carriage that brought them here. The man arguing with her looked like an official of some sort, probably an officer of the law. He wore the same uniform as the two back at the carriage—light armor, green and gold tunic, and a single pauldron with a raised emblem strapped on the left shoulder. He carried a sword that hung off to one side. His blonde "pretty boy" look disappeared as he scowled with disgust, arguing with Alyssa.

The man next to him looked more like a scribe than a lawman. He gripped a satchel tight against his chest, seemingly afraid to act or speak up as his large, floppy chaperon hat hung down across his face. He had to push up his wire-rimmed glasses as they fell off his long, thin nose.

The law officer grabbed the paper out of Alyssa's hand and tossed it over his shoulder without a glance. She went to pick it up, but he shoved her aside, knocking her down to the ground. That's when Malcolm had seen enough.

There was a fire in him, making him move without thought for his own well-being. He rushed to the mantel and picked up his weapon. It was a .44 caliber Dunkhurst Magi-Rifle, a sharpshooter long rifle capable of firing ten rounds adaptable for six magical arts. Malcolm instinctively snapped the lever, like he did every day for more than thirty years in the war, loading a bullet into the chamber. Although his mind was still confused about many things, one thing was clear to him: Alyssa was in danger, and he would not stand by.

He ripped open the door, startling everyone. Without a word, Malcolm leveled the rifle at the man who had pushed Alyssa. "*Gaoth!*" he said as he fired, lowering his aim to the ground beneath the man's feet. He pulled the trigger, and a gust of wind shot out. Upon impact, the ground exploded like a twister, sending the lawman flying through the air.

He turned his weapon toward the scribe, but the timid man held up his hands and backed away. "Please, don't hurt me!" he pleaded.

Malcolm lowered his weapon before turning his attention to the other two. They drew their swords and started to rush him. Malcolm cocked the magi-rifle, chambering the next round before taking aim. "*Dealanaich!*" he said as he pulled the trigger, this time sending a bolt of lightning arcing through the air. The bolt hit their swords, causing them to drop them instantly from the stinging sensation. The last threat eliminated, Malcolm cocked his weapon again before moving over next to Alyssa.

"Are you alright?" he asked, helping her to her feet. She was overjoyed, knowing that he had come out to save her like he always did.

"I am now," she said as she picked up the paper before getting to her feet. Malcolm watched as the other two helped the blonde-haired man up. As they huddled together, Malcolm leveled his magi-rifle.

"Come near my wife again, and I'll make you regret it!" he said as he cocked the hammer back. The lawmen lingered, knowing full well what a magi-rifle could do. A single word enchantment could imbue magic from the ether into the bullets with devastating effects. Magi-Gunners were specialists in long-range magical warfare, and Malcolm was one of the best.

"Excuse me, are you Malcolm Seger?" the gangly scribe spoke up for the first time. "Who wants to know?" Malcolm asked, his attention still trained on the three lawmen at the end of his rifle.

"I do!" came a voice from behind the carriage as a lone rider approached the homestead. A cloak of green silk with a peacock feathered collar flowed effortlessly behind the horse that carried a knight in full plate mail with ease. The same emblem from the lawmen's pauldrons were etched proudly on the knight's chest plate—a phoenix soaring out of the sun—

the signet of Fawleen. His gray hair shone in the morning sun just as brightly as his armor. Everything about this knight demonstrated his intimidating presence and overall authority.

He stopped next to the carriage. Without a word, one of the lawmen ran over and took his horse by the reins, steadying the animal as the knight climbed down. He strode over to Malcolm and Alyssa, the blonde lawman jumping to his side.

"Sir Aleister, I can explain—"

"Dalton, I told you to wait for me before coming up here," he said without looking at him. "If you can't follow my orders, then perhaps you need to find another line of work."

Dalton hung his head and stepped behind Sir Aleister. Malcolm lowered his magi-rifle, laying it across his arms as he stood with Alyssa behind him. His legs were weak, but he pushed himself to stand firm to protect her.

"Are you Malcolm Seger?" Aleister inquired.

"I am, and you are?"

"Sir Aleister Cornwall, Lord Marshal of Fairhaven," he replied. Malcolm knew not to take the title of Lord Marshal lightly. These were the representatives of the Crown in each parish across Fawleen. "And you, miss? Your name?"

"Alyssa. Alyssa Seger," she meekly replied with a curtsey.

"I see . . . You do know that the Crown forbids marriage between humans and the Dragonkin of Drogon in Fawleen – "

"I am a citizen of Fawleen," Alyssa interrupted. "I earned my place by serving during the war. Furthermore, Lady General LaPorta herself sanctioned our union."

"Don't interrupt the Lord Marshal with your lies, newt!" Dalton snapped at her, using a known racial slur against Dragonkin. Immediately, Malcolm leveled his rifle at Dalton, right over the shoulder of the Lord Marshal. The startled deputy took a step back. In his weakened state Malcolm could barely hold the weapon up with one hand, but his anger kept him strong and steady.

"Call my wife that name again, and Lord Marshal or no Lord Marshal, I'll kill you where you stand!"

Dalton quivered as he looked down the barrel of the magi-rifle. Sir Aleister used a single finger to push the weapon away.

"You must forgive my deputy," he said. "He's new to the job and doesn't know his manners when dealing with newcomers." Aleister just glared at Dalton, who took a step back and lowered his head again. "Now, do you have your certificate of citizenship and marriage, Mrs. Seger?"

Alyssa held out the papers she had tried to show Dalton earlier. Sir Aleister took them and handed them over to the scribe. "Assessor, did you scan the seals to confirm their veracity?"

"No, Lord Marshal," the assessor stuttered as he took the papers. "Deputy Stalwart was adamant that they were forgeries—he never allowed me to scan them."

"Really," Aleister murmured as he glanced back at Dalton. "Well, as I said, my deputy is new to the job and needs further instruction in proper procedure." While he spoke, the assessor took out a tablet and a glass optic from his case. As he worked, Aleister turned his attention back to Malcolm and Alyssa.

"I believe the land grant office told you to bring this documentation to the magistrate's office upon your arrival in Fairhaven, yes?"

"I have been ill for the past month from exposure to Dragon Dust. Alyssa's been taking care of me," Malcolm explained to the best of his ability. The revelation surprised everyone involved.

"Dragon Dust? Where did you come across it? Here?" Aleister inquired. Malcolm didn't know how to answer his question, so Alyssa spoke up.

"We were unpacking our belongings, and there must have been some residual spores on his coat. I treated the men and women of our brigade in the war, so I was able to cure him before he succumbed to its effects."

Her answer satisfied the Lord Marshal, who turned his attention to the assessor. He opened the documents and placed his optic over the seal. A runic circle formed, and a magic-enhanced seal appeared above the lens. It glowed with a bright pulse in the same phoenix emblem as the signet of Fawleen.

"The citizenship paper is official," the assessor said, handing it back to the Lord Marshal. He opened the second paper and repeated the procedure. This time an emblem of a shield and crossed spears appeared above the lens. It was the seal of the Lady General of Fawleen.

"As is this one," he said, concluding his review of the documents. "Alyssa Antoinette Fantasia Seger is a citizen of Fawleen, and the Lady General Celeste Augustina LaPorta approved her marriage to Malcolm Reginald Seger."

"Well then, everything appears to be in order," the Lord Marshal confirmed with a smile. "We just need your seal to record you as residents of Fairhaven. Do you have it with you?"

Before Malcolm could answer, Alyssa touched him on the shoulder. "I know where your seal is, Malcolm. I'll go and get it for you."

As she headed inside the house, Malcolm continued to face down the Lord Marshal. "So, you are a Magi-Gunner?" Aleister inquired.

"Was. I'm retired now," Malcolm answered succinctly.

"What regiment were you with?"

"55th King's Musketeers, Zephyr Brigade," he answered.

Aleister's shock at the mention of the famed unit flashed across his features.

"You were at the massacre at Chronost Pass? That was one of the bloodiest battles of the war. You survived that ordeal?"

"Alyssa and I were the only survivors from our regiment," Malcolm explained with a hint of sadness in his voice. "We lost all of our friends-our family-that day. And you, Sir Aleister? What regiment did you serve in to earn the title of Lord Marshal?"

Before Aleister could answer him, Alyssa returned, carrying a small wooden box. She opened it up, revealing a golden seal. Malcolm took the box, handing Alyssa his magi-rifle. The assessor placed a drop of wax on a document and recorded their names.

"Place your seal here, Master Seger," he instructed.

Malcolm placed his seal on the wax and pressed down. He felt a tingle as magic from the ether passed from him through the seal and onto the wax. When he pulled it back, a magical circle with his signet appeared above the wax seal. It was the signet of his unit—crossed magi-rifles surrounded by a vortex of wind.

When they completed the process, the assessor rolled up the document and placed everything back in his case. "Let me be the first to welcome you to Fairhaven," Sir Aleister said with sincerity, holding out his hand to Malcolm. "I look forward to seeing you in town soon." Malcolm took his hand to shake it, but his legs finally gave out and he stumbled slightly. Alyssa quickly grabbed him under the arm, taking his weight upon herself.

"If you would like, I can ask Doctor Tomlin to stop by and check on you," Aleister said with a voice of concern. "I do not doubt that your wife provided you with excellent care, but you can never be sure when it comes to Dragon Dust."

Malcolm looked at Alyssa, who nodded her head in agreement. "That would be fine. Thank you, Sir Aleister."

The Lord Marshall gave a slight bow before he turned to leave. Dalton sneered in silence as he followed behind him. Alyssa ignored him and quickly moved to help Malcolm back inside.

"You pushed yourself too hard, Malcolm," she scolded him. "You probably depleted what little mana you had by doing that. You need to rest to allow the ether to restore you completely."

"I couldn't let that bastard get away with treating you the way he did," he replied. "Besides, all the action helped me in more ways than you can imagine."

"What do you mean?" Alyssa asked curiously.

"My memories are becoming crystal clear, Alyssa, but I need you to help me piece it together."

"Of course, but how can I help you?"

"I need you to tell me what happened to me," he began. "I wasn't exposed to Dragon Dust spores left behind on my coat. I need you to tell me the truth, Alyssa."

Alyssa understood what he was asking of her. It might be hard for him to hear, but she knew if they were going to move forward, he needed to know everything. "Alright, let's go eat our breakfast and get you settled, then we'll talk."

Outside, Dalton was desperately trying to get back into the good graces of the Lord Marshal. "Sir Aleister, I know I shouldn't have acted on my own as I did, but I was trying to get ahead of the situation," he explained. "How can we be certain that those papers are authentic? You wouldn't want a Drogon spy coming into our parish, would you?"

"Dalton, the seal of the Lady General of Fawleen, let alone the King's seal, cannot be forged," Aleister chided. "As far as I'm concerned, Alyssa Seger is a citizen of Fawleen and deserves to be treated as such."

"How can you say that after everything you did as a part of the Bloodfist Brigade to stop the Dragonkin from destroying Fawleen?"

Aleister was becoming frustrated with his young deputy. "What I did was a part of the war, and the war is over, Dalton. The Dragonkin, for the most part, are now productive citizens of Fawleen—at least those that sided with us in the war. We cannot abuse or ignore their rights because of bias."

"But sir, to have that newt living here amongst us, it's just unnatural!"

"I would be careful continuing to use that name around here, Dalton," Aleister warned. "Of all the King's Musketeers, I know from excellent sources that Malcolm Seger was one of the top-ranked Magi-Gunners. He killed the Drogon General Shabaz Hellstrim with a single shot to the head at a distance of nearly twenty kels." Dalton swallowed hard as he looked back toward the house. "As long as they abide by the law, I suggest you leave Malcolm and Alyssa Seger alone," Aleister concluded. "You're only asking for trouble."

As Aleister rode off ahead, Dalton climbed into the carriage, staring back at the Seger house. He would never truly accept their presence in Fairhaven. The Drogon had killed his father and older brother in the war, and he would never allow the Dragonkin to take hold in his country. No, Dalton Stalwart would do everything within his power to force them out of Fairhaven.

Malcolm and Alyssa sat down to eat their tepid breakfast. Alyssa wanted to start making a proper hot meal again, but Malcolm talked her out of it. He didn't mind the lukewarm eggs or soggy toast. It reminded him of the many quick meals they had eaten during the war, but deep down, it also reminded him of something else.

At a diner just off the turnpike, he had worked in the kitchen during the late-night shift. Far removed from warring humans and dragonkin, Malcolm recalled diners sending back their food if their eggs were cold or their bacon soggy. There was a part of him not of this world.

Malcolm sipped his coffee while Alyssa washed up the breakfast dishes. He offered to help, but she told him in no uncertain terms to stay out of her kitchen. Malcolm knew they were going to talk about things, but he couldn't wait. He had a gut feeling about what had happened, but he needed her to confirm it. For his sanity, he needed to know the truth.

"Alyssa," he said, getting her attention. "What happened to me?"

She kept on washing the dishes, trying to ignore his plight a little longer. "I told you, exposure to Dragon Dust caused your illness, and I nursed you back to health."

"No, Alyssa. I mean how did I die?" His response snapped her to her senses as she slowly looked over at him. Malcolm could tell, from the look in her eyes, that his gut feeling was confirmed. "I have two memories inside my head," he continued. "I remember being Malcolm Seger, Fawleen Magi-Gunner fighting in the Endless War. And I remember meeting you, fighting alongside you, and falling in love with you.

"All of those memories are here," Malcolm added as he pointed at his head, "and here," then to his heart. "But there are other memories too. I remember being a cook in an all-night diner just off the New Jersey turnpike, working a late-night shift just to make ends meet. I worked, went home, and worked some more. I had no family, no friends, and no life to speak of at all. But then, I remember an accident on a rainy night, dying by the side of the road, and when I woke up, I was here.

"These are memories of another place, another time, another world, and they're slowly fading away as the memories of Malcolm Seger take over. So, before they're gone completely, I need you to tell me what you know, for my peace of mind. Who am I, what happened to me, and how did I end up here with you?"

Alyssa sighed, realizing that his memories were more intact than she imagined. She put the last dish down and wiped her hands dry before walking over and sitting across from him at the table. She took a sip of her coffee, then began to speak.

"We moved to Fairhaven a little over a month ago," she began. "We took our pension from the war and bought this place away from the cities hoping that we could get a fresh start. But unfortunately, our home was in desperate need of some work, so we took our time fixing it up.

"We soon found the well blocked. The pump only brought up a trickle of water when there was plenty down there. So, you climbed down to investigate. That's when the Dragon Dust got to you. They saturated the bottom of the well."

"What? Here? But how, why?"

"During the war, the Drogon overran this area," Alyssa explained. "They hid something down in the well and dumped Dragon Dust down there to prevent humans from recovering it. That's what was blocking the pump. You had it with you when I pulled you out."

"What was it?" Malcolm asked. Alyssa got up and went over to the chest on the other side of the room. She unlocked the trunk and pulled out something wrapped in cloth. She brought it over to the table and set it in front of him. Malcolm put his cup down and unwrapped the tightly woven cloth to discover a sword. It was less than three feet long with a thick round ricasso and a dragon ruby embedded in the center. The double-edged blade had a dragon head for a pommel. Malcolm recognized it immediately, as he had seen one before during the war.

"That's a dragonslayer," he exclaimed. "What in God's name is a dragonslayer sword doing here?"

"As best as I can tell, the previous owner was slain by the Drogon when they ransacked this region, but they didn't want to take the sword with them in fear that it would be recaptured by Fawleen and used to kill more Dragonkin. So instead, they dropped it down the well and dumped Dragon Dust down there to prevent anyone from recovering it."

"I'm not sure if I'm comfortable having this here with you," Malcolm said as he wrapped the sword back up.

"Malcolm, if there's anyone I trust with this sword, it's you," Alyssa said as she took it back over to the chest. "It's only useful if you know how to find a Dragonkin's second heart." One of the reasons the war had taken so long was because Dragonkin have two hearts—a regular heart and a magical heart. If you did not destroy both, the Dragonkin would live on and continue to fight. But the dragonslayer sword took that factor out of the equation. If you stabbed a Dragonkin through their magical heart with this sword, it killed them instantly.

It had been the Oracles of Delphis Kai that revealed this secret to Fawleen. They had helped the humans develop the dragonslayer weapons on the promise that, after the war, they would destroy them to ensure others would not exact revenge on the remaining Dragonkin. Their goal had been to end the war, not commit genocide on their race. After the war, as promised, the King of Fawleen had ordered all dragonslayer weaponry melted down.

"I was going to turn it over to the Lord Marshal once you got better, but after seeing that deputy today, I am having second thoughts."

"I don't blame you, and I agree," Malcolm concurred. "We just need to keep it hidden, for now. So, I went down the well, became exposed to the Dragon Dust, and I'm guessing you couldn't save me in time, and I died."

Alyssa sat back down, nodding her head as a tear rolled down her cheek. "The well was such a tight, enclosed space. It concentrated your exposure to the Dragon Dust. You were dead before I could cast any magic to save you."

"So, what about this spell of restoration you mentioned?"

Alyssa paused before she answered. It was not that she was afraid to tell him the truth, but rather, she did not know precisely how to explain it. "The spell of restoration does what it says . . . It restores life to the dead."

"So, it's a type of holy resurrection?" Malcolm surmised. "But I thought that was impossible?"

"It is. Resurrection magic is impossible without the caster sacrificing part or all of their soul to bring back the dead. That is why the Oracles of Delphis Kai developed the spell of restoration. It takes two souls and merges them into one."

"So Malcolm Seger's soul merged with someone else, but who? Who am I? Not someone from Fairhaven?"

"No, no one locally. The spell taps into the boundless cosmic lifestream—we call it the River of Souls—and finds a compatible soul willing to be reborn into a new life, a new world. It's a form of reincarnation, but one that stretches across time, space, and worlds."

Malcolm searched his memories, piecing together everything Alyssa had told him, and it all fell into place. His recollection merged until he finally knew the truth. "I could hear you," he admitted. "I heard you crying out in the rain, asking God not to leave you alone."

His statement shocked Alyssa. She hadn't told him about that, and yet he knew what she'd said. "You heard me?"

"It must have been raining, both here and in the world I originally came from before. I guess the angels were crying that night. My body became crushed beneath the metal wreckage of the car that hit me."

"A car? What is that?" Alyssa inquired. Malcolm tried to put it into words she would understand.

"It's like a mechanized carriage, without horses," he explained. "Anyway, I laid there, dying, and I could hear someone crying, praying not to be left alone. I couldn't see you, but I could hear you. Across time and space, I heard you cry out and asked God not to let my life end there on that lonely road. I wanted to do something with my life. I didn't want you to be alone."

Alyssa could not help but cry-the tears streamed down her face. Here was someone she had never known, someone who had reached out across the infinite to be with her. Alyssa had fallen in love with Malcolm Seger over years of blood and battle. And now, she fell in love with him again. It only took a matter of days to get to know this new incarnation of him. He had given up his place in heaven to be by her side.

She got up from her chair and, without even thinking, sat on his lap and laid her head against his chest as she continued to cry tears of joy. It caught Malcolm off guard, but he became overwhelmed with the emotion of the moment. He wrapped his arms around her, careful to avoid her wings and tail as he shed a few tears himself.

After everything that had happened earlier that day and the years of war they endured together, Malcolm knew he had to be there for Alyssa. He had never found love in his old life. He had prayed for God to give him a chance, and here he was.

Alyssa sat up slightly to look Malcolm in the eyes, cradling his face with her hands. "You came for me," she muttered through the tears. "You heard my prayer and crossed the River of Souls to be with me."

Malcolm reached up and wiped the tears from her eyes. "I would die for you," he said without hesitation. "I don't remember a lot about my old life, except that I was always sad and alone. I know how that feels, Lyssa, and I will do whatever it takes to make sure you—I mean we—we are happy, both of us, together forever!"

Alyssa laughed through the tears as she heard a familiar voice talking to her. "You called me Lyssa!" she cried. "Only you ever called me Lyssa!"

He smiled, and then Malcolm leaned in and kissed her softly and lovingly. She hesitated at first, but her emotions overwhelmed her, and she responded in kind. Alyssa wrapped her arms around his head, pulling them closer. Their loving embrace rekindled what they had shared before, but for a part of Malcolm, it was a new sensation too.

Alyssa leaned her head against his. "So, what do we do now?"

"Now? Now, we do what we came here to do. We make a home, maybe start a family, whatever we want." His words caught Alyssa off guard. They never discussed a family before, as humans and Dragonkin had never married before. The idea of children had never crossed her mind.

"A family? But we never talked about a family. I don't even know if we can conceive a child. And there's the shame and humiliation they would go through being a mixed breed. I don't know if I want to put a child through that!"

Malcolm heard her concerns, and he understood every one of them. He remembered times of racial hatred and strife from his old life, and the bigotry against the Dragonkin was just as intense. Still, something deep down said he needed to stand up for their love and their life together.

"When I was a little boy, my mother ran off with another man, so my father raised me alone. He worked hard to make sure we had a roof over our heads and food on the table. Beyond that, he found solace at the bottom of a liquor bottle, so I was on my own a lot. There was, however, one time he said something to me that I will never forget.

"I had gotten into a fight at school, defending a friend being bullied by this group of older teenagers. I was hurt pretty badly and ended up in the hospital. While I lay in my hospital bed, my father rushed in, screaming my name at the top of his lungs. It scared me to death, thinking he would scold me or yell at me, but that wasn't the case. When he found me, tears were streaming down his face. He hugged me . . . He had never hugged me before that day. I was shocked.

"After I told him what had happened, he just looked at me and told me how proud he was of me. He told me that I must always stand up for what I believe in, and I did that to help my friend. Acting without a conscience is not acting at all. You must always be on the right side of every fight because that is the only thing worth fighting for."

Seeing the look of confusion on Alyssa's face, Malcolm decided to be a little more straightforward with her. "I will always fight for what is right, including your right to be a mother, because I know you would make a great one. You're the most caring, loving person I've ever met. The best way we can overcome fear and prejudice against the Dragonkin is by showing them our love and our resolve in starting a family."

"We can speak to the doctor when he gets here about whether or not we can conceive a child," he continued. "After that, we'll just let nature take its course. If it happens, it happens. If not, then we'll just grow old together in this house."

"You do realize that my lifespan differs from yours?" Alyssa interjected. "I'm not even middle-aged, and you are, well, as you like to say, past your prime!"

"Nonsense, you're only as old as you feel, and since half of my soul is that of a 24-year-old, I feel like a new man. I have my whole life ahead of me." The two shared a laugh, something neither of them had done for quite a long time. It was the medicine they both needed.

Their laughter was interrupted by a knock on the door. Alyssa gave Malcolm a peck on the lips before she got up and walked over to the door. A rather distinguished-looking gentleman met her with thinning white hair on his head but a very thick beard around his chin.

"Good morning, I'm Doctor Anthony Tomlin," he said with a slight bow, gripping a large straw hat in one hand and carrying a medical bag in the other. "Lord Marshal Cornwall asked me to stop by to check on Malcolm Seger." He looked at Alyssa over the top of a pair of sunglasses. Alyssa was impressed with how neat and suitably pressed he looked in his white suit. She recognized the badge over his breast pocket—the signet of Fawleen held within open hands. It was the symbol of a licensed medical doctor of Fawleen.

"Yes, of course Doctor, please come in," Alyssa said as she waved him in. "I'm Malcolm's wife, Alyssa."

"Yes, the Lord Marshal told me about you so I wouldn't be surprised when I got here. It's nice to meet you, Mrs. Seger."

"May I take your hat?" she asked politely. "Would you care for some tea or coffee?" Alyssa was nervous. She had never received guests before, so she desperately tried to follow the usual courtesies she had either read about or experienced in her travels around Fawleen.

"Oh, yes, thank you, tea would be lovely," he said as he handed her his hat before sitting down at the table next to Malcolm. "And how are you feeling, Mr. Seger?"

"Still a little weak, Doctor Tomlin, but Alyssa's been taking good care of me. She was our regimental healer during the war."

"Well, that's rather convenient . . . for you, I mean. I met my wife under similar circumstances," he recalled, shocking both Malcolm and Alyssa.

"You served in the war, Dr. Tomlin?" Malcolm inquired.

"Yes, I was the regimental physician for the 78th King's Cavaliers, Dreadknight Brigade. My wife, Lily, was one of my nurses. Fortunately, when the Dragonkin Oracles took over front-line duty for old country doctors like me, I was relegated to hospital duty for the remainder of the war. The rest, as they say, is history."

"I hope you don't hold that against me or my kind, Doctor," Alyssa interjected when she handed him a steaming cup of tea.

"Thank you, my dear, but no, quite the contrary. Working as hospital staff allowed me and my wife to get to know each other better and start our family. It also saved my boys from having to serve in that God-awful war. No, I am eternally grateful for your service to Fawleen."

Alyssa smiled as his kind words lifted her heart after the earlier skirmish with the deputies. It seemed some humans did not share their race's intense animosity toward the Dragonkin. After a few more minutes of friendly conversation, Dr. Tomlin gave Malcolm a thorough examination and concluded he was satisfied with his care and condition.

"Well, it seems that the Lord Marshal's concerns were all for naught," he commented as he put away his medical equipment. "You are in excellent health, but mind you,

Dragon Dust exposure can come back from time to time. So don't overexert yourself for the next few weeks. We'll need to see how your body copes with it."

"You can rest assured that I will make sure he doesn't do too much too fast, Doctor," Alyssa said. "The sphenophyllum leaves I add to his tea help to fight off the effects of the Dragon Dust."

"Sphenophyllum? But those plants are a deadly poison!"

"Only the roots are, Doctor, not the leaves," she explained. "I pluck the leaves, dry them and then crush them to use in tea and other healing elixirs. I found that it helped our squad fight off fever and infections from the poisons infused into Drogon weapons."

The doctor was astonished by her medical revelation. "Remarkable! Does it also work on other diseases and afflictions?"

"It can, but you have to be careful when it's administered to someone new. Malcolm has been taking it for years, so he has quite the tolerance for its effects. You have to gradually increase its dosage, over time, to let the body adjust to the medication."

Alyssa went over to her cabinet in the corner of the kitchen. She pulled out two small pottery jars with cork stoppers. Alyssa handed one to Doctor Tomlin. "Here are some extra leaves I dried and ground. Please, take them with you and try it out yourself. I recommend using a jelly spoon to measure it out. I find that works best. Start with one spoonful mixed with regular tea leaves in a tea ball with one cup of hot water daily. Then, add an extra spoonful every few days, but don't exceed four spoonfuls. Any more than that can make the tea bitter and sour the stomach."

He took the jar from her and looked at it curiously. "I typically find that medicine isn't supposed to taste good."

Alyssa was shocked to hear a physician say that. "Then how do you get your patients to take it?" she responded, making the Doctor question his reasoning. "And here, this is for you!" she said, handing him the second jar.

"What's this?" he queried, taking it from her.

"It's a skin cream to help protect you from sun exposure. I use it on my tail to keep it from drying out, and I thought it could help you."

"But, how did you know I have a skin condition?"

"Your hat and sunglasses, for one. Older people usually wear them to protect them from the sun," she observed, "and when you sat down to examine Malcolm, I could see the blotches on your head. They must be painful. What do you use to treat it?"

"Oh, usually a mixture of palm oil, honey, and turmeric. It's an old family remedy."

"Well, try this. You may find it works better on your delicate skin," Alyssa advised him. The doctor opened the jar, took a sniff, and poked his finger inside before rubbing the thick cream between his fingers.

"What do you use to make this?"

"Now, now, Doctor Tomlin . . . I can't give away all my secrets!" she smirked slyly. "If you need more, just stop by again. I'd be happy to provide more as a thank you for taking the time to check up on Malcolm."

Doctor Tomlin placed the two jars in his bag before getting up to leave. "Well, if these remedies of yours do work, I would be very interested in purchasing more of them from you to use in my practice," he offered. "I realize that some people in Fairhaven may be reluctant to seek out such a talented healer like yourself, so this could be an opportunity for you to have a less formal introduction."

Alyssa thought about it for a moment, then looked to Malcolm for advice. He nodded his encouragement, realizing this could be a great chance to take the first step toward acceptance with the people of Fairhaven.

"I would be happy to provide you with some of my elixirs and remedies, but give me a few weeks to replenish my supplies. I haven't been able to forage since Malcolm fell ill."

Doctor Tomlin grinned, happy to have a good source of remedies at his disposal without having to go through regular apothecaries.

"One more thing, Doctor, if you don't mind?" Malcolm began, getting his attention. "Do you have any knowledge of conception, or lack thereof, between humans and Dragonkin?"

The doctor looked at Malcolm and then Alyssa, who turned red with embarrassment. "Well, several studies conducted during the war varied in their final analysis," he explained. "When male Dragonkin from Drogon, well, raped human females, the children born were usually deformed and died shortly after birth. These irregularities were associated with the chaos magic frequently used by the Drogon.

"The few *reported* assaults by human males against female Dragonkin were inconclusive because most of the women died after they became pregnant," he concluded, "killed either by their kind out of intolerance or by their human assailants, worried about siring a half-breed."

Doctor Tomlin could see that his answer had succeeded only in confusing his young patient. "In my own professional opinion," he added, "humans and Dragonkin are compatible biologically. To me, the only thing that matters is the love of the home that a child is born into. Should such time ever arise for you, Mrs. Seger, my wife is an excellent midwife and would be happy to assist you."

Both Malcolm and Alyssa were overjoyed to hear such heartening news from Doctor Tomlin "Well, if and when the time comes, I will be grateful for her help, and yours as well, Doctor Tomlin."

"Excellent! I'll be back to see you in a few weeks!" With that, Doctor Tomlin put on his hat and sunglasses as he left.

Malcolm was happy to see Alyssa come out of her shell. It was like when she had first joined the Musketeers. Most of the squad had kept their distance at first, but Alyssa had made her presence known through her healing arts. She had become a vital part of the Zephyr Brigade, and she had done it all on her own.

Though he still felt a bit weak, Malcolm pushed himself to rise from the table without assistance. Alyssa sighed as she rushed to his side. "You're just desperate to hurt yourself today, aren't you?" she reprimanded.

"I don't like feeling helpless, you know that. So I need to push myself to get back to a hundred percent."

"How about you rest for now and try some more tomorrow?" she offered. "You did a lot this morning, Mal, and I'm so proud of you, but please, let's take it easy for the rest of the day, okay?" Malcolm chuckled under his breath, which confused Alyssa. "What's so funny?"

"You called me Mal . . . only you ever called me Mal!" She smiled and gave him a tender kiss. It was only a nickname, but it meant more than that. The two were finally coming to a better understanding of their relationship and their future.

Months had passed since his rebirth into this world, and Malcolm was enjoying every day of his new life with Alyssa. They spent their days working on fixing up their home and their nights working on their relationship as husband and wife. Even though most of Malcolm's memories had returned to normal, a part of him still felt lost in his surroundings. He had read every book on hand as well as some new ones he purchased in Fairhaven, covering every subject imaginable. He also reread his diaries from the war to focus on memories of people, places, and his life before rebirth.

Mostly though, he just wanted to spend time with Alyssa. They talked about everything from war and politics to poetry and music. For both of them, it was like getting to know each other all over again. They took it slowly, not wanting to rush things. Even though they slept in the same bed, they decided to forgo intimacy, for now, waiting for the right time. For them, it deepened their relationship and their love.

They kept a small garden in the back of the house. In addition to vegetables and herbs, Alyssa grew flowers that bloomed beautifully, filling the air with sweet scents year-round. While Alyssa tended her garden, Malcolm repaired its fence to keep the animals out. He looked up from time to time, watching as Alyssa pulled weeds, plucking and clipping what she needed. Malcolm remained in awe of this beautiful woman. His heart raced every time he looked at her. *How anyone could object to being around her is beyond me! These people are so ignorant of the real beauty in this world.*

"You're doing it again." Alyssa's words broke his trance.

"What do you mean?" he asked, looking away as he went back to his work.

"You're staring. I hate it when you stare at me. It can be a little unsettling sometimes."

"Well, I heard a preacher once say 'look to the image of God which, by its beauty and dignity, should allure us to love and embrace one another,'" Malcolm replied with a smirk. Alyssa chuckled loudly at his shoddy excuse.

"My God, you are such a flatterer," she joked. "You used the same line on me when we were on furlough at Dol Finnegan, remember?"

"It worked, didn't it? And sometimes you have to stick with what you know," Malcolm said with a wink.

"Yes, well, a girl likes to hear something new every once in a while," she said with a pout, picking up her basket of herbs and vegetables and turning to go to the house, but Malcolm's voice stopped her in her tracks.

"Love is a language that all creatures can understand.
It's the only thing that can transcend realms —
a spell anyone can cast or fall for —
the most powerful enchantment there is.
Beings call love 'magick,'
but there is no one recipe for it.
And that's what makes it beautiful."

He surprised Alyssa with a perfect recitation of one of her favorite poems. It took her breath away to hear him deliver it so eloquently. Malcolm had never been one for poetry, but he had gone out of his way to impress her. She walked over to the fence and caressed his face, kissing him tenderly. It shocked her that something so simple could move her like that.

"When did you take an interest in poetry?" she asked.

"Well, I know how much you like it, so I bought a book the last time I went into Fairhaven," he replied, pulling a small book from his back pocket. "I thought it might come in handy should I ever slip back into my old habits. Besides, I'm beginning to enjoy reading it. Though I'm mostly just looking forward to reading *yours* someday."

Alyssa loved poetry so much that she had started writing her own during the war. It was how she had coped with the death and destruction around her. "Oh, my work is nowhere near the quality of the poem you just recited."

"It's not the quality that counts, Lyssa. As long as it comes from the heart, that's all that matters." She felt reassured by his kind words and his confidence in her.

"Well, I better get working on these medicines for Doctor Tomlin. I'll have the next batch ready for you to take down to his office by this afternoon," she reminded him.

"Lyssa, why don't you come with me?" Malcolm asked, causing Alyssa's face to turn sour. "Mrs. Tomlin has been begging me to bring you down so she can finally meet you face-to-face. We could make a day of it–see the sights, go shopping at the open market–what do you say?"

"I don't know, Mal. It's been a long time since I've been to a large city. I'm just not very comfortable with the idea yet."

"All the more reason for you to come with me," he explained. "Everyone in Fairhaven knows that I am married to a Dragonkin, and their curiosity increases every time I walk into town. Maybe it's time to prove their fears wrong. Come on, don't make me beg."

As much as she would like to continue to object, Alyssa just couldn't say no to his reasoning. Maybe it was time to confront the fear–both hers and theirs. "Alright, but I'll need a little more time to get ready. I look a fright."

"No you don't, but that's your prerogative. You go do what you need to do and I'll finish fixing this fence so those marmots stay out of your garden." She gave him another kiss and turned to leave. This time, though, Malcolm grabbed her by the tail before she took a step and gave it a yank. Startled, she quickly smacked his hand away.

"What have I told you about yanking on my tail? It's very sensitive!"

"Which is why I do it!" he retorted, laughing but smiling very seductively at her. She wanted to be mad, but she couldn't help smiling back at him. She loved his playfulness. It helped ease the tension she felt about going into Fairhaven, which she knew was exactly why he'd done it.

Alyssa took her time, finishing the medicines and packing them properly before getting ready for her first trip to Fairhaven. She picked out her best dress and did her hair and makeup, doing everything she could to make the best first impression. Malcolm gave her space, which Alyssa appreciated. The last thing she needed to hear was "hurry up" or "you look fine," which would only increase her anxiety. After a few hours, she finally picked up her basket of medicines and went outside to find Malcolm.

"Malcolm?" she called, looking around for him. She had expected to find Malcolm sitting on the porch waiting for her, but she didn't see him anywhere. Suddenly, she heard a loud whining sound, like the howl of a banshee. Alyssa ran off the porch and around the house to see where the sound was coming from. She noticed the barn door was wide open—the strange sound seemed to be emanating from within.

Like a wild stallion bursting from its stall, Malcolm rode out of the barn on something unexpected . . . an Etherzine Land Cycle! It stretched out with twin steel forks holding a single wheel in the front and two large wheels in a row under the driver's seat. The whirring sound came from the jet engine on the front end. It sucked in air and converted it to energy to propel the Cycle at incredible speeds. The air around them vibrated with the power and sound of this superb machine.

Land Cycles were used primarily for couriers during the war because the Drogon couldn't catch them nor replicate their mechanics. In a country town like Fairhaven, they were impractical due to the rolling hills and winding country roads, especially for inexperienced drivers. Fortunately, Malcolm had some experience driving a Land Cycle.

He wore pieces of his old uniform for protection and comfort—a long leather coat, pants, vest, and boots—with a pair of goggles over his eyes. He had a .357 Spellcaster strapped to his hip. These handguns were favorites of Magi-Gunners in close-quarter combat, capable of the same effect as the long rifles. He raised his goggles, grinning from ear to ear, thrilled that he was able to surprise her.

As Alyssa's shock at the sight of the Land Cycle wore off, she tried to get Malcolm's attention over the roar of the engine, but he couldn't hear her. Finally, he shut it off so they could talk.

"Where in God's name did you get a Land Cycle?"

"Old man Harley gave it to me in place of payment for the work I did on his roof," Malcolm explained. "His son was a courier during the war, but he left the Cycle behind when he took a job with a shipping company in the southern archipelago. And besides, we could use some reliable transportation."

"A horse is reliable transportation, not a Land Cycle."

"It's quite reliable if you know how to drive one, and I do," Malcolm assured her. "Besides, I've always wanted one. Trust me, it'll be fun!"

Alyssa thought about it for a moment, and against her better judgment, she decided to take a chance. "Alright, but take it easy please? I don't want any of these medicines to break on the way there," she said, handing him the basket. Malcolm got down and opened up the compartment under the back seat. He gave her a pair of goggles and placed the precious cargo inside.

Malcolm straddled the Land Cycle, but Alyssa was not sure how to do that in a dress. "How do you expect me to ride on that in a dress?"

"You sit side-saddle, just like you would ride a horse," he explained. "Keep your wings folded tight against your back and wrap your arms and your tail around me. You'll be just fine."

Alyssa did as he instructed, sitting on the seat with her legs hanging over the side. She wrapped her arms around him tightly and then her tail, leaning into his back. Alyssa was a little intimidated by the machine but being with Malcolm eased her fears. It even took away some of the anxiety she was feeling about going into Fairhaven.

Malcolm started up the Land Cycle and the engine roared to life. "Okay, here we go!" he shouted, putting the Land Cycle in gear and speeding off away from their home. The wind rushed by as they sped down the open road toward Fairhaven. At first, the sudden burst of speed startled Alyssa, but then she settled in and it was exhilarating. The twists and turns of the road and the constant beating of her heart excited Alyssa. She let out a scream of joy and laughter. It was music to Malcolm's ears. He loved to make her happy and see her smile, and she was very happy right now. Her life before now had been one of profound sadness with only intermittent sparks of happiness. Malcolm wanted to change all of that.

There were a few bumps along the way, but overall their ride into Fairhaven was uneventful. They passed farms and homesteads all busy with activity. Seeing a Land Cycle speed past them caused curiosity and the occasional wave, especially from children playing.

It was the first time Alyssa had been to Fairhaven since they moved to the area. She had only seen it from the outside.

The buildings were half-timbered brick houses with sloping slate roofs and small balconies overlooking the streets. Colorful banners stretched across the city streets and down the sides of buildings displaying the city's pride in Fawleen and victory in the war.

There were war posters still partially hanging, which gave Alyssa a shock. Pictures of knights standing over dead Drogon warriors were the prevalent theme in most of them. Their purpose was to inspire courage and support enlistment in the war effort. But for Alyssa, it was a statement of hate and distrust of the Dragonkin. She saw that same look of distrust in the eyes of the people as they sped through the streets. As they drove around the town, she questioned letting Malcolm bring her to Fairhaven.

Doctor Tomlin's office was located just inside the town square. Most of the crowded square overflowed with carts and stalls for the weekly open market. People filled the marketplace, buying everything from fresh fruits and vegetables to jewelry and woodwork items. With the plaza so crowded, Malcolm parked the Land Cycle on a side street away from the activity.

"We'll have to walk to the doctor's office from here," he told Alyssa as he shut off the Land Cycle. He helped her down off the bike before stepping down himself. Malcolm whipped off his goggles and tossed them under the seat and pulled out the basket of medicine. He passed it over to Alyssa, but she ignored him. All she could do was stare out into the square, looking at the eyes staring back at her. The people of Fairhaven watched her, whispering amongst themselves, making her uncomfortable with every passing moment.

"Alyssa, don't worry about them," Malcolm said, snapping her out of her trance. "They don't know you as I do."

He handed her the basket, and his smile reassured her. Alyssa felt at ease, and she took the basket from him before handing over her goggles. He clasped her hand in his and looked into her eyes. "Remember, I'm right here with you."

He held out his arm, and Alyssa smiled as she took it. They walked together through the marketplace, not worried about the people's glaring eyes or muffled comments. Malcolm wanted to show the people of Fairhaven that they had nothing to fear from Alyssa. Most people ignored them or just gave a polite "hello" or nod as they passed. For the most part, they didn't know what to make of a Dragonkin living amongst them.

From the doorway of the *Haven's Roost* tavern, Deputy Stalwart leered at the two of them. He was the only one intently watching their every move. Dalton hadn't expected Malcolm Seger to bring his Dragonkin into Fairhaven. With this development, the deputy tried to calculate his next move.

Malcolm and Alyssa crossed the square without issue and reached Doctor Tomlin's door. He kept his office on the lower floor of the building while he and his wife lived in the second-floor apartment. It was a lot of space for just two people but afforded plenty of room when their children and grandchildren came to visit. Once inside, Alyssa got her first opportunity to meet Doctor Tomlin's wife, Lily.

"Just a minute! I'll be right with you!" shouted a lively voice from the back room as the bell above the door rang. Malcolm and Alyssa stepped into the small waiting area. The sparse room furnished with simple chairs and tables and sporting walls plastered with colorful floral wallpaper made it look more like a child's nursery than a doctor's office.

"Now, what can I do for you?" Lily Tomlin asked as she walked into the waiting room. She had a spring in her step and a youthful stride that complimented her smooth skin and muscular physique. Alyssa was surprised at how different she appeared compared to Doctor Tomlin. Her mahogany skin set off her stark white hair. Lily showed off her vim and vigor by wearing short-sleeve dresses cut above the knees. She was very proud of her healthy regime and used her appearance to profess the benefits to others.

"Oh my goodness, you're here!" she exclaimed. Lily was elated to see Alyssa with Malcolm and, without any hesitation, went over and gave her a big hug. Mrs. Tomlin's reaction stunned Alyssa, who gingerly returned the embrace. "I was hoping you would make the trip into Fairhaven. It's so good to finally meet you, Alyssa!"

"Thank you, Mrs. Tomlin," she replied. "It is nice to meet you too!"

"Now, now, none of these 'Mrs. Tomlin' formalities," she interrupted. "You must call me Lily."

"Alright, Lily," Alyssa said, so taken aback by Lily's overwhelming acceptance of her as a Dragonkin that she forgot her reason for being there. "Where is Doctor Tomlin?"

"Ah, it's his fishing day," Lily said with a wave of her hand. "Once a month he takes a day off to go fishing, and yet he always comes home empty-handed. I think he does it just to get away from me." Malcolm chuckled under his breath, earning him a sharp elbow from Alyssa.

"Oh, here are some fresh supplies for Doctor Tomlin." Alyssa handed Lily the basket brimming with jars of medicines, elixirs, and herbs, which Lily was ecstatic to see.

"Did you happen to bring the Willow Bark cream?" Lily inquired. Alyssa reached into the basket and pulled out a jar, handing it to her, bringing a smile to her face.

"Wait here!" she said, taking the basket of medicine with her into the back. Within moments, Lily returned, escorting a young lady carrying a small vial of the cream. She was barely out of her teens, not the type of person who needed medicine for rheumatism.

"Audrey Lynn, this is Alyssa Seger. She makes the Willow Bark cream for your mother," Lily announced. Immediately, the young lady went over and took Alyssa by the hands. She didn't hesitate for one second over the fact that Alyssa was a Dragonkin. Her appreciation was bursting out as tears of joy streamed down her face.

"Oh, Mrs. Seger, thank you so much!" she said, shaking her hands vigorously as she thanked her profusely. "My mother would be bedridden with pain if it wasn't for your cream. She is finally able to do her needlepoint and sewing again, which makes her so very happy. I can't thank you enough."

Alyssa was shocked by the overwhelming gratitude. It was the first time she had felt appreciated for her work as a healer in quite a long time. "Oh, please, no thanks are necessary. I'm just glad it works so well for her. And if you ever need more, and Doctor Tomlin is out, please don't hesitate to come by and see me."

Malcolm was delighted that Alyssa was coming out of her shell. She seemed so alive and outgoing for the first time since the war—exactly how he had hoped her life would be—a part of society, not an outcast.

"My mum's in the market today, selling her needlepoint and other hand-sewn items," Audrey continued. "If you get a chance, please stop by! I know she would want to thank you herself!"

"Oh, rest assured, we will," Malcolm interjected before Alyssa could say anything. He knew it was a little pushy for him to volunteer her like that, but he wanted his wife to experience people who looked past the racist overtones brought on by the war.

With one last wave, Audrey left with a bounce in her stride. Alyssa stood in the shop, still flustered by everything the girl had said. Even her friends during the war had never appreciated her as much as Audrey had just now. She was elated by the exchange; it gave her newfound confidence in herself.

Lily brought out a small pouch of coins, giving it to Alyssa. "Here's the money for your medicine. Go buy yourself something nice in the market." Alyssa took the bag of jingling coins with a smile and handed it to Malcolm, but he just stepped back, holding up his hands to refuse.

"Oh no, you earned that," he exclaimed. "That's all yours, Lyssa. Besides, you're better with money than I am."

"Well, that's true," Alyssa joked as she put the pouch in her pocket. "Thank you again, Lily. I hope we'll be seeing each other again soon."

"We'd better!" Lily said, giving her another hug and a kiss on the cheek. "Don't be a stranger . . . You're welcome here anytime."

As Malcolm and Alyssa left, he noticed a new spring in her step that mirrored her joyful spirit as they headed back into the market. She wasn't holding back like before. Instead, Alyssa returned salutations and greetings with more than a simple nod of her head. She was openly conversing with people, her smile as bright and beautiful as her personality. Alyssa was glowing, and Malcolm noticed how other people's attitudes changed when she talked with them at each stall. They relaxed as if their fear of the Dragonkin faded away with every word she spoke.

Malcolm became so distracted with his own shopping needs that he didn't notice Deputy Stalwart quickly approaching Alyssa amidst all the excitement. Flanked by two of his subordinates, Dalton stalked his way through the market until he found Alyssa, stepping between her and the local farmer with whom she was chatting as she selected apples to purchase.

"There's nothing for you to buy here," Dalton exclaimed, putting his hand up to the farmer, glaring as the intimidated man backed away. "Nobody in this market will sell anything to you."

Alyssa was frightened at first, but her blood boiled at the gall of this deputy. "This is a free market! You have no authority to tell these people who they can and can't sell to!" she argued.

"When it comes to Dragonkin, I have every right! You don't belong here with humans! You're nothing but trash!"

"I am a citizen of Fawleen! I fought to bring an end to the war! Where did you fight, hm-mm? Tell me, Deputy Stalwart, what did you do during the war?" Alyssa argued with Dalton, his anger intensifying toward the Dragonkin as she insulted his integrity.

"I'm here to prevent newts like you from ruining our-" A fist came out of nowhere as Malcolm suddenly charged forward and hit Dalton square in the jaw. The deputy flew backward into his men, which kept him from falling to the ground.

"I told you before—never call my wife that name again!" Malcolm said. The two lawmen went for their swords but stopped when Malcolm drew his Spellcaster, cocking back the hammer. "Do you want to go through this again?"

The two men immediately released their swords and stepped back. They remembered the lighting attack from their first encounter, still feeling the stinging sensation on their hands. However, Malcolm's aggressive stance didn't faze Dalton, and he immediately drew his sword. "Striking a deputized officer of the crown; that'll earn you time in a jail cell, Seger!" he said.

"I didn't hit an officer of the crown," Malcolm retorted. "I hit a bully abusing his authority and attacking my wife for no reason!"

"No reason? She's a Dragonkin, and her very existence is reason enough!"

"The war is over, Deputy Stalwart, and we won thanks to Dragonkin like Alyssa and the other Oracles of Delphis Kai. They gave up their homeland, their people, family, and friends to help us defeat the Drogon Empire because they knew how evil and corrupt it was. They were victims of the Drogon too—because they wouldn't submit to their dark chaos magic—just like us."

"We are nothing like them!" Dalton interrupted.

"Oh yes we are!" Malcolm countered. "You would know that if you ever got to know them. Alyssa's people took the place of our doctors and clerics on the front lines so that people like Doctor Tomlin and his wife, Lily, could fall back to serve in the hospitals, survive the war, and serve the people of Fairhaven. Without their support, I doubt we would have won. Our fathers, mothers, sons, and daughters would still be fighting and dying through the 'Endless War' if it hadn't been for them.

"The Dragonkin that survived are now a part of Fawleen. They eat, breathe, live, laugh, and love just like we do," Malcolm concluded as he took Alyssa by the hand. She smiled and kissed his hand, stepping close to him. "So, if you want to continue fighting the war, you go right ahead. But as for my wife and me, the war is over. We're here to live in peace, but make no mistake—I will not let you bully the people of Fairhaven nor us into falling in line with your sick, twisted point of view."

Dalton sneered at Malcolm's "lies." But what truly concerned him was the growing voice of the people in the market. They were listening to Malcolm and agreeing with his argument. In Dalton's mind, Malcolm was turning the people against their kind. That was the worst kind of sedition.

Just then, the farmer that had been helping Alyssa picked up the bag of apples and handed them to her. "Here you go, Mrs. Seger!" he exclaimed, looking right at Dalton as he gave her the fruit. He was not afraid of her, nor intimidated by Deputy Stalwart. Suddenly, others in the marketplace spoke up, vying for Alyssa's attention. A tear rolled down her cheek as she was overwhelmed by the support of the people of Fairhaven.

Meanwhile, Deputy Stalwart's rage only intensified. "I'm placing both of you under arrest for assaulting an officer of the crown and criminal sedition!" he screamed.

"No, you're not!" came a voice from behind. Stalwart froze in fear as he turned around to see Lord Marshal Cornwall walking toward him. His intense stare put Dalton in his place as he strolled into the market. "Sheath that weapon, now!" he commanded. Deputy Stalwart slowly and reluctantly put his sword away. "Now, I want the three of you back in the office. You're relieved of duty!"

"But Sir Aleister, I was only—" Lord Marshal slapped him across the face, cutting short his excuses and shocking everyone in the square.

"I don't want to hear another word out of you, Dalton! Get back to the office! That's an order!"

Dalton rubbed his cheek as he looked at the people gawking at him, some even laughing under their breath. But the worst was when he looked over at the Segers. They had a look of pity on their faces. That was the last thing Dalton wanted from them.

He took off, leaving the square in shame with his two subordinates following close behind. After they departed, Sir Aleister walked over to Malcolm and Alyssa as the marketplace returned to normal. "I find myself continuing to apologize for my deputy, dear lady, but this time he went too far. It was my failure to reign him in that led to this confrontation."

"No, Lord Marshal, there's no need for you to apologize," Alyssa said with a polite curtsey. "Some people are still holding onto the same bigotry that started the war in the first place. While others," she continued as she motioned around the square, "learn from past mistakes and embrace the possibility of change."

"Well, in any case, I can promise you it won't happen again," Aleister stated as he politely bowed before reaching out his hand to Malcolm. "And thank you, Malcolm Seger, for showing restraint toward my deputy. I know things could have gotten out of hand. I appreciate your tempered approach."

"Well, if there's one thing Alyssa has taught me, it's when to fight and when to talk," Malcolm explained as he took the Lord Marshal's hand. "With all these people around, I didn't want it to escalate into a full-fledged brawl."

"I wish my subordinates had the same common sense. Would you mind if I called on the two of you tomorrow? There are some things I would like to discuss further once I deal with my wayward deputy."

Malcolm looked to Alyssa before he answered. She nodded. "Please come by tomorrow afternoon for tea," she offered. Sir Aleister gave a courteous bow and headed off to deal with his misguided deputy.

"So, what should we do now?" Alyssa asked.

"I think we need to do some more shopping," Malcolm said. "These people are itching to sell you something, and we may get some good bargains in the process." The two laughed as they continued walking through the crowds of people in the marketplace. Every booth and stall tried to catch their attention and sell them something. It was a fantastic turn of events. In one day, the people of Fairhaven moved past their fears and regressed hatred and finally put the war behind them.

As night fell, the forest filled with the sparkling lights of a thousand fairy flies dancing in the moonlight. After a successful shopping day, Alyssa cooked a delicious meal of rare tri-horned bison and fresh-baked apple pie. The mouthwatering aroma filled the house, even after they had finished

their meal. After dinner, Malcolm and Alyssa settled down for their usual nightly routine.

They sat in front of a roaring fire, warmed by the crackling logs in the hearth. Alyssa sat on one side of the sofa, writing down her thoughts and poetry in a leather-bound journal while Malcolm sat at the other end, reading a book and sipping on 50-year-old Sundinian Bourbon. They gave each other a little personal time every night to indulge themselves in their own passions.

For Alyssa, it was writing her poetry. The day's events in Fairhaven had inspired her, so Alyssa put pencil to paper and wrote down her thoughts and feelings as soon as she could. Her poetry was her escape mechanism-how she dealt with the horrors of war and people's bigotry toward her and her kind. But today was different. She had seen another side of humans that she had previously only experienced through Malcolm and the others in their brigade.

"I see today's activity has inspired you, yes?" Malcolm inquired. He'd been enjoying watching her eyes widen with delight as she wrote down her poetry.

"I am," she replied. "Today was miraculous, and I never want to forget this feeling. Putting it into words will help me remember."

"Can I hear what you've written so far?"

"Malcolm, you know I don't like anyone to see or hear my poetry," she replied. "It's just not good enough."

"Then why do it if you don't want to share it? Poetry should be heard, not hidden away. And besides, how do you know if it's any good if you don't let anyone read it?"

"I know, I know, it's just . . . I'm afraid of what people will say. It's hard enough being a Dragonkin in human society without having them judge my poetry too. That's a little too much for me."

"Well then, how about you start with just me," Malcolm offered as a compromise. "Read me one of your poems as a start."

"Oh Mal, I don't know . . ."

"Come on, Lyssa, I'd love to hear one. How about the one you wrote after the battle of Chronost Pass? You worked on that one for weeks while we recovered in the hospital. Would you please read it to me?"

Alyssa sighed, frustrated at the pressure he was putting on her. But she finally relented, hoping that reading it would stop him from asking in the future. She started paging through her journal until she found the poem. "Just promise me you won't say anything until I finish reading, alright?"

Malcolm just nodded his head as he put down his book to listen.

"We begin and end battles with 'cries.'
We rush towards the enemy with our voices loud

with our battle cries

determined to defend our beliefs and stance.

In the end, we hear the cries of the wounded

yelling for help.

A dying plea to any savior willing to show up.

For those skilled or lucky enough to survive,

visions of death haunt the people of the Battle of

Chronost Pass.

It was the kind of battle

where you recognize the faces of your enemies

while standing close enough to smell their last meal.

Where you take life after life after life

with no time to think between killing blows.

No spells could prepare us for the loss.

No enchantments could prepare us for devastation.

No oracle could prepare us for the heartache.

Just like melted down dragonslayer weaponry,

the blood in our veins boiled with the horrors of war.

When the last of the weapons were laid on the ground,

we could finally breathe again.

It didn't take more than a few breaths to realize

the fight wasn't over.

Every day, from Dragon Dust to dawn,

we fight to protect our hearts,
our magic, and our future legacy."

Alyssa didn't look up until she finished reading her poem. When she finally looked over at Malcolm, hoping he wouldn't be too critical of her work, she saw something she had never expected. Malcolm was crying.

His face was flushed and tears streamed down his face. The memories of that day, the battle they had gone through, the death of his family . . . his friends. It was overwhelming; Alyssa's poem perfectly captured the emotions of that day. Malcolm's emotions got the better of him as he broke down.

Alyssa put her book down and went over to him, cradling his head in her arms as she tried to console him. This was the first time she had seen such a reaction, especially to one of her poems. She had similar reactions when she read the varied works of her favorite poets, but this was much different. It was personal for them. This poem represented a part of their history together.

"I take it you liked it," Alyssa joked as she wiped the tears from his eyes and kissed him softly on the forehead. Malcolm responded by holding onto her tighter. When he finally composed himself, he let her go so they could look at each other.

"Don't ever think your poetry isn't good enough," he said. "It was beautiful. Your words turned this big, burly man into a sobbing little girl."

"Maybe not a little girl, more like a big teddy bear!" They both laughed, but the laughter disappeared when they looked into each other's eyes.

"With every word, it was like reliving Chronost Pass all over again. The pain of battle, the sorrow of losing our friends, and the joy of surviving that day with you. You have such an amazing heart, Lyssa, like no one I've ever known," Malcolm continued. "Your words—your poetry—are as powerful as the magic you used to bring me across the River of Souls. I am so proud to stand by your side and call you my wife. You are my love . . . my life."

Alyssa placed her hand on his cheek, letting her thumb graze the contour of his mouth. She slowly leaned in and kissed his lips. The taste of him was inviting to her, one of woodsmoke and bourbon with a hint of musk. Malcolm held her tight, his senses overwhelmed by the smell of her sweet perfume combined with her natural pheromones. He pulled her down with him as he laid back on the sofa, leaving a trail of kisses down her neck and across her sternum. The months of repressed emotion built up after his rebirth and the two falling in love all over again were finally released in this single moment.

They made their way to the bedroom. The couple took their time undressing each other, touching and kissing as they let the passionate fire build inside them. Their skin ignited with the tingling sensation of each stroke of a finger or kiss on the flesh, reinforcing their desires. The two lovers let their bodies dictate their lovemaking. They didn't want to stop, didn't want to let the other go, no matter how exhausted they felt. This night was theirs, to be together as one.

Malcolm was a gentle lover to Alyssa. Her wings and tail made their lovemaking a challenge, but he didn't care. Malcolm knew how to please Alyssa without hurting her or making her feel uncomfortable. For them, all that mattered was being together.

When they finally fell asleep in each other's arms, drained but content, the lovers curled up under the sheets. Malcolm held her close as she laid her head across his chest. Alyssa listened to the rhythmic beating of his heart as it lulled her to sleep. Malcolm, comforted by the warmth of her body, rested his hand behind his head and slowly dozed off. He had finally found peace in this new life—in the love of the woman lying next to him.

As the sun rose into the morning sky, a trickle of sunlight shone in through the windowpane. Alyssa stirred from her slumber as the warm glow struck her face. She rolled over, reaching for Malcolm, but he was already out of bed. Typically she was the first to awaken, but last night had left her completely exhausted. She touched the bed where Malcolm had lain. It was still warm, reminding her of the heat from his body as he had lain with her. Her heart skipped a beat as she recalled the love they had shared last night.

Her thoughts were interrupted when she heard the clanging of dishes coming from her kitchen. She realized what Malcolm was doing, and that terrified her even more . . . He was cooking. Quickly, she jumped out of bed and got dressed before rushing out.

As she walked down the hallway, the smell was intoxicating—a combination of sweet custard and warm spices. Alyssa had never smelled anything like that before. It actually made her mouth water. When she reached the kitchen, Malcolm was standing over the stove with a hot griddle plate, dropping pieces of egg-soaked bread onto it. He was happy, almost giddy, whistling as he worked on preparing breakfast.

Alyssa smiled when she saw him so energetic, but then she remembered to be angry with him. "I thought we had an understanding?" she said, getting his attention. "The kitchen was my domain, and you were to stay out of it!"

"Yes, we did agree to that, but I wanted to surprise you," Malcolm said as he continued to work on breakfast. "Please, sit down; breakfast is just about ready!"

"I'm beginning to wonder if you still have memory loss," Alyssa snapped playfully as she strolled over next to him. "Malcolm, I love you, but you, dear husband, are no chef." She looked down at the egg bread he was grilling, and the smell was even better than before. "What on earth are you making?"

Malcolm just smiled, knowing full well he had piqued her interest like a spider catching a fly in its web. "Why don't you sit down and see for yourself?"

Alyssa finally relented and went over to the table, sitting down. She was unaccustomed to being served like this, and it made her a little uncomfortable. Still, Malcolm was happy, and the food he was cooking did smell good, so maybe there was something to this. The table was already set with a kettle of tea sitting under the cozy. *He really thought everything through.*

Malcolm put the last of the egg bread onto a plate before reaching into the oven and pulling out a cast-iron skillet. He grabbed the plate and brought both over to the table. He set the grilled custard bread down first before placing the skillet on a hot plate. It was a baked egg mixture filled with meat, vegetables, and cheese. Alyssa had never seen anything like it before.

"What is it?" she queried.

"French toast with an egg frittata," Malcolm exclaimed as he sat down across from her. He carefully cut the frittata, like a piece of pie, and placed it on her plate, followed by two slices of French toast. "Now, we don't have any maple syrup, so I made a cloudberry compote to pour over top." Carefully, he poured some of the sweet berry liquid from a tiny pitcher over her French toast.

Alyssa looked at the plate of food, wary of eating it, remembering Malcolm's previous attempts at cooking. Still, it smelled delicious, and she didn't want to disappoint him. She carefully cut a piece of the "French toast," as he called it, ensuring she got some of the cloudberry jam on it. Alyssa slowly placed it in her mouth, expecting the worst but genuinely surprised at how delicious it was. The flavor was sweet, rich and filled her mouth with custardy goodness. She immediately went for another piece to see if it was a mistake, but that bite was just as good as the first.

Alyssa then cut into the frittata and tasted it. The savory flavor of egg, meat, and cheese with the perfectly cooked vegetables was a taste sensation. When she finally looked over at Malcolm, he just sat there grinning as he poured the tea. He was so full of himself, proud of his accomplishment, but happy that Alyssa enjoyed his food.

Alyssa used her napkin to wipe her mouth and swallowed her food before addressing his pompous attitude. "Okay, how did you do this, Mal?" she asked. "This is not your regular cooking!"

Malcolm couldn't help but laugh before answering. "I told you that in my previous life, in the other world, I was a short-order cook at an all-night diner."

"A diner?"

"A restaurant," he answered. "We were open all day and all night, serving travelers along a busy highway. I worked the 'graveyard shift' from late at night until early in the morning. Our specialty was breakfast, so I got really good at cooking everything from pancakes, waffles, and French toast to omelets, eggs any way, and a killer frittata.”

“Well, if you can cook this well, perhaps I should let you cook breakfast more often.” Alyssa was impressed with his cooking, and the fact that his merged memories from his other life still remained. Perhaps that was what had changed him from the man she first fell in love with into this new man sitting here with her today. It made her love him even more.

“If you think this is good, wait until you taste my cinnamon rolls! They are to die for!”

The two laughed some more as they enjoyed their breakfast together, taking another step forward in their relationship. The melding of souls was more than the spell Alyssa had cast to revive Malcolm. It had brought the two of them closer together.

Malcolm spent at least an hour a day performing maintenance on the Etherzine Land Cycle. He wanted to keep it in top performance, ready to go at a moment’s notice. Once he had seen one in action during the war, he was hooked: the thrill, the speed, the power of the machine. But that wasn't the only reason. There was something there from his other life.

He remembered restoring a 1948 Indian Chief motorcycle. It was a barn find that was begging to be brought back to life. He had spent every extra dollar he earned on spare parts and tools needed for the project. He had wanted to take his time restoring a classic.

Malcolm felt the same way when he first saw the Land Cycle. It was a streamlined work of art and raw power. When old man Harley offered it to him, Malcolm just couldn't say no, and restoring it to working order was a labor of love.

"Malcolm!" Alyssa called as she walked into the barn, breaking his concentration. "Sir Aleister will be here soon. You should come in and clean up!"

"Alright, I'll be in shortly," he replied, his arm elbow deep into the engine housing. "I'm trying to replace the ether filter, but the damn thing is stuck. I've almost got it."

"You know, sometimes I wish you'd touch me as much as you do that Land Cycle."

Malcolm turned his head and looked at her with a sly grin. "Funny, I don't remember hearing you complain about that last night?" he joked. Alyssa smacked him on the shoulder and laughed along with him.

"Well, just hurry up," she added. "I'll go put the kettle on."

Malcolm continued his work until he finally got the old filter out. Now came the hard part of putting the new filter in. As he resumed his work, he heard footsteps approaching the barn. "I'm almost done, Lyssa!" he said as he felt a shadow fall across him, but it was bigger than his wife. He looked out of the corner of his eye to see Sir Aleister standing there with his horse.

"Sorry to disappoint you, but I'm not your wife," Aleister joked. Malcolm locked the filter in place and stood up.

"My apologies, Sir Aleister, but Alyssa's been on me to finish my work and get cleaned up before you got here," Malcolm explained as he wiped his hands off and offered one to the Lord Marshal. "It took me a little longer than expected to replace that damn ether filter."

"That's why I prefer a horse to a Land Cycle. It requires little maintenance and is less time-consuming," he joked.

"Yeah, but not as much fun to ride," Malcolm shot back. "Here, you can tie her up in here. It looks like it could storm later." He took the reins and led the horse over to one of the stalls, providing some hay and water before leading the Lord Marshal into the house.

Alyssa entertained their guest while Malcolm freshened up. She set out fresh tea, cakes, and biscuits for the Lord Marshal. When Malcolm finally joined them, the three sat down around the table to enjoy their afternoon tea.

"So, what happened to Deputy Stalwart, if I may ask?" Malcolm started the conversation, earning him a side glance and elbow bump from Alyssa for being rude.

"Well, I dismissed him and his two friends. I cannot allow deputies under my authority to act like they are above the law. They left Fairhaven this morning, but that's not why I asked to speak with the two of you. There's something you need to know about me."

"Oh? And what's that?" Malcolm queried.

"You asked me before where I served in the war to earn my position as Lord Marshal of Fairhaven," Aleister began. "To tell you the truth, I was embarrassed to tell you before, but I can't hide the fact any longer. I was a member of the 5th King's Praetorian Guard, Bloodfist Brigade."

That name sent shockwaves through both Malcolm and Alyssa, but none more than Alyssa. She knew the name of the Bloodfist Brigade all too well. In the early days of the war, whenever the Fawleen Army had taken over an area of Drogon, the King's Praetorian Guard had been responsible for law and order within that region. They had ruled over the Dragonkin with an iron fist, ruthless and unforgiving, and none had been more brutal than the Bloodfist Brigade. They were legendary for putting down countless rebellions and counter-insurgencies by the Drogon. The body count of this brigade alone exceeded all others combined during the Endless War.

Hearing that name, Alyssa leaped to her feet and screamed at the Lord Marshal. "How dare you!" she cried. "How dare you come into my home and sit at my table, knowing full well the blood of thousands of Dragonkin rests on your hands! You monster!"

Malcolm put his hand on Alyssa's arm to try to calm her down, but his own anger boiled inside him. Still, he wanted to hear what Sir Aleister had to say. "Alyssa, please, let's hear him out," Malcolm said to try and calm her rage. "I think there's more to it than just that."

Alyssa tried to catch her breath, quelling the anger inside her. Finally, she sat down, but she turned away from the Lord Marshal, refusing to even look at him. Aleister took a deep breath, relieved that he had even gotten that out, before he continued.

"Everything you say is true, Mrs. Seger. We were monsters. The king put us in charge of the border towns that we conquered, knowing full well we would keep the Dragonkin in line with harsh, cruel tactics. And for the longest time, I had no problem with that. I was doing my duty for King and Country, but the longer the war went on, the more I realized that I wasn't.

"Once the king brought in the Oracles of Delphis Kai to join the fight, many of my comrades were reluctant to accept a Dragonkin amongst us, but we obeyed the king's edict. The one to join my brigade was Bors Dumont."

When Alyssa heard that name, it shocked her, and she again looked at the Lord Marshal. Aleister saw in her eyes that she knew him. "Did you know Bors?" he asked.

"He was my mentor at the abbey," she admitted.

"He was a remarkable individual. No one else would spend time with him, but I was always one to try and understand those we were fighting against. So, I sat down and talked with him. We spent many long hours engaged in discussions of life, philosophy, and religion. He was quite insightful, and he opened my eyes to have a better understanding of the Dragonkin. And then . . ." he paused, unsure of how to continue as he took a sip of tea.

"And then?" Malcolm interjected, egging him on.

"And then we arrived in the village of Sgothan Heights," Sir Aleister finally continued. "We were ordered to investigate the mountaintop village as a possible outpost for Drogon scouts. The high altitude made it the perfect spot for spying down on the Killian Plains. You could see for a hundred kels in any direction from that plateau. But when we got there, all we found was a simple village of worshippers of Delphis Kai. They were peaceful and welcoming. In fact, Bors' uncle was the village chief."

"So what happened?"

"I thought we would leave the village in peace, but my comrades had other ideas. They decided to take their frustrations with the war out on the villagers. They separated the male Dragonkin from the females, especially the young females. My protests to my comrades fell on deaf ears, so I sought out my commander. I found him in a home with several of our other senior officers. They . . . they were taking turns with a young female Dragonkin. She couldn't have been more than eighteen years old.

"I stood there and watched as they ravaged her. The look in her eyes, the sheer terror, plunged a dagger into my soul. She reminded me of my own daughter at that age. It was horrifying . . . and then I snapped. I drew my sword, and one by one, I killed all of the senior officers. I found Bors and told him to attend to the young lady while I dealt with the rest of the brigade. I went around the village and killed them, one at a time. I left none alive."

His admission shocked Alyssa and Malcolm. Typically, an act like this would constitute treason, but somehow, this went unnoticed. "How did you cover something like this up?" Malcolm asked.

"Bors and I sat down with the Chief and other elders of the village. As much as they appreciated saving their young females from my men, we all knew it would bring about the wrath of Fawleen. So, we developed a plan. They had some pieces of Drogon armor and weapons. We put them on the dead Dragonkin who resisted our earlier efforts. Bors even took his uniform off and put it on another Dragonkin. To most humans they all look alike, so no one would know the difference."

Alyssa sat there, mouth agape, at the revelation. "Master Bors is alive?" she inquired.

Aleister simply nodded his head. "The villagers gathered what they could, and then we set their homes on fire. We had to make it look like a Drogon sneak attack destroyed our brigade and the village. I even had Bors run me through, but he did it with precision so I wouldn't die from my wounds–

although I wish I had. In any case, I would be the only survivor."

"So that's why Dalton and the others flocked to you," Malcolm interjected. "They believe you're this hero of Fawleen, slayer of Dragonkin, but it's all a façade." Aleister simply nodded. "So what happened to the rest of the villagers?"

"I forged the proper paperwork, and they resettled as refugees in the southern archipelago, on the island of Dawntree. That's the island the king gave to the Oracles of Delphis Kai as a new home," he explained. "They had to change their names, of course, to ensure no one could trace them back to Sgothan Heights. Bors calls himself Bjorn now."

Aleister reached into a pouch at his belt and pulled out a leather-bound journal. He opened it and ripped out a piece of paper, handing it to Alyssa. "Here's his full name and address. I'm sure he'd love to hear from you." Alyssa smiled for the first time since the Lord Marshal's revelation. She was ecstatic to learn that her former friend and master was still alive. It was then she noticed a picture sticking out of his journal. It was a picture of a Dragonkin woman.

"Who is that?" she queried, not wanting to be rude, but her curiosity got the best of her. Aleister pulled out the picture and handed it to Alyssa. It showed a young Dragonkin female sitting on a rock overlooking the sea. All you could see was her brilliant smile, happy to be alive in her new home.

"That is Chandra, the young lady I saved," he explained. Alyssa admired the photo before handing it back to him. "She writes to me from time to time, letting me know how she's doing. She's seeing someone, a carpenter. They hope to be married next spring. She asked me to walk her down the aisle since all her family was killed at Sgothan Heights, but I told her no. I couldn't take the chance of anyone discovering our secret."

The old knight was sullen and heartbroken as he spoke. Alyssa could see how much it meant to him. "Sir Aleister, I don't know if I can forgive all the atrocities you committed against my people," she began, before pointing to the photograph, "but she has, and that's all that matters. You not only saved her life but the lives of all the people of that village. You went against your king and country for the sake of your soul. That says a lot about a person."

Her kind words touched the Lord Marshal, who dabbed a tear from his eye with his fingertip. Malcolm understood how difficult it must have been for Sir Aleister, not only living a lie amongst the people of Fawleen but living with the guilt himself. Malcolm thought there might be a way to boost his confidence and show the Lord Marshal they trusted him. He got up from the table and went over to the sideboard, pulling out the wrapped dragonslayer sword. Malcolm set it down in front of Sir Aleister, who had a distinct look of confusion about him.

"What's this?" he questioned.

Malcolm sighed before sitting back down. "It's the real reason I became infected with Dragon Dust," he explained. "We weren't sure about giving it to you with Deputy Stalwart around. Now that he's gone, I think this will be safe with you."

Aleister untied the wrappings, revealing the dragonslayer. Malcolm explained about finding it at the bottom of the well and the dose of Dragon Dust protecting it. The Lord Marshal appreciated the trust they both placed in him by giving him this sword. "I am truly grateful for the faith you have in giving me this sword. I know it's not easy, especially for you, Mrs. Seger. But rest assured, I will see to it personally that this weapon is destroyed."

The three continued their afternoon tea, talking about other things than the past. With everything going on, they failed to hear the soft sobs just outside their window. Dalton stood there, eavesdropping on their entire conversation. He was heartbroken that the man he considered an idol, role model, and hero had turned out to be nothing but a fraud. He realized he had to deal with these traitors, and he knew just how to do it.

After an hour, the clap of thunder echoed across the sky, bringing them to their senses. The Lord Marshal finished his last sip of tea. "Well, I should be going," he said, dabbing his mouth with the napkin. "Thank you for the tea and cakes, dear lady. Everything was delicious."

Alyssa nodded politely with a courteous smile. She was still conflicted about her feelings toward Sir Aleister, but she would put it aside for now. Malcolm was a little more understanding and polite toward the Lord Marshal. "Let me walk you out, Sir Aleister," he said, getting up quickly.

"No, no, thank you, Malcolm," Aleister said with a wave before he picked up the dragonslayer sword. "There's no need for both of us to get soaked. I appreciate the two of you listening to me today." With a bow, the Lord Marshal departed. Once the door was closed, Malcolm looked over at Alyssa as she cleared the table.

"You were a little rude to the Lord Marshal, don't you think?"

Alyssa shrugged, giving him a sideways glance. "I'm sorry, Mal, but it's tough for me to be anything but coarse with that man," she explained. "Do you remember when we passed through the village of Stelmar? There was practically no one left alive. And the stories they told me of how the 'Bloodfist Brigade' treated them, it was horrifying. I can't believe the king gave that man the title of Lord Marshal, besides the fact that you gave him the dragonslayer sword."

"I did, and I'll tell you why," he started to say, but first, he strolled over next to Alyssa and pulled her close. He didn't want to fight with her about this, so he needed her to understand his reasoning. "When I look at him, I don't see a mass murderer. I see a man desperately seeking redemption. He is living with his past, and it's tearing him up inside. He sees you—sees us—and we give him a glimmer of hope that his sins can be forgiven. That's all he wants."

"I know, I know, it's just so hard for me to forgive him."

"In my other life, there was a passage from the Bible I remember hearing in church. I remember it because it reminded me to keep my nose clean and not follow others down the wrong path. The pastor said, 'The thief comes only to steal and kill and destroy; I have come that they may have life, and have it to the full.'"

Alyssa was confused by his curious recollection. "I don't understand?"

"It means beware those ungodly people that wreak havoc on those around them, but through God, you can seek salvation from an eternity of suffering and sin," Malcolm explained. "His penance is living with the truth of what his brigade did. He's carrying their sins by living. From what I've heard, the Lord Marshal spends every waking moment outside his duties at the cathedral in prayer. Through prayer, he is seeking redemption of those sins through God, and in effect, through us too. Who are we to deny him that?"

Alyssa contemplated everything Malcolm had said. His heart was in the right place, as it always was. He was such an optimist, looking for the best in people, while Alyssa was a consummate pessimist, never knowing who to trust. They balanced each other in their relationship. That's what made them so perfect together.

A clap of thunder roared outside as the rain began to fall, but it couldn't cover up the loud whinny of a horse or the guttural scream of pain. Malcolm and Alyssa raced outside to the barn, worried that something had happened to Sir Aleister. When they reached the barn, they found the Lord Marshal lying on the ground, bleeding from a stab wound in his abdomen. He held both hands over the wound to try and stem the bleeding, but the pain was too great for him.

"Sir Aleister!" Malcolm screamed as he rushed to his side. Before Alyssa could help, a shadowy figure grabbed her from behind and placed a blade across her throat. She looked down at the edge and trembled in fear. It was the dragonslayer sword in the hands of Dalton Stalwart. He held her tight, keeping her wings and tail pinned, just like his brother showed him when fighting a Dragonkin. The blade scratched her and blood trickled down the metal's edge. It sent shivers through her body as the cold steel cut her.

Malcolm instinctively reached for his .357 Spellcaster hanging on his Land Cycle, but the holster was empty. From across the barn, Dalton's two cohorts stepped out, swords in hand. One of them had Malcolm's weapon tucked into his belt. Malcolm knew there was no fighting them. His first concern was Alyssa and Sir Aleister.

"Damnit Dalton, at least let Alyssa help Sir Aleister! Otherwise, he'll bleed to death!"

"Serves him right!" Dalton snapped back. "He deserves a traitor's death, killing his men and siding with the damn newts! He is a false hero, and he'll die like one, just like you and your newt whore!"

Malcolm started to rush Dalton, but the other two leveled their swords at him. He stared at the sharp blades, wondering if he could get past them to save Alyssa, but with the dragonslayer at her throat, he knew it was a lost cause. He would have to bide his time, for now.

"Let's go outside, so the traitor can die alone!" Dalton ordered, motioning for Malcolm to move outside. Malcolm couldn't leave Sir Aleister in such a state, so he quickly knelt beside him and wrapped the Lord Marshal's cloak around his abdomen, tying it tightly to try and stem the bleeding. Sir Aleister pulled Malcolm close and whispered something to him before Dalton's men pulled him to his feet. They shoved him out of the barn and into the pouring rain. The two kept their swords aimed at Malcolm while Dalton slowly pushed Alyssa outside.

"What did he say to you?" Dalton inquired.

"He said not to worry about him and save my wife."

Dalton laughed. "Sorry to disappoint you, but there's nothing you can do to save your pet newt. You're going to watch her die right before your own death. Then I'm going to travel to Dawntree and kill that newt harlot and the rest of the Dragonkin from Sgothan Heights who should have died that day. I will be revered as an avenger for all humankind by wiping the Dragonkin from our world. And it's all thanks to you, Seger! By saving this dragonslayer, you will be the one responsible for their genocide! What do you have to say to that?"

Malcolm said nothing, quelling his anger to keep his mind focused. "Just this . . . Before this storm passes, I'm going to kill you and your underlings!" he said. Then he reached out and grabbed the grip of his Spellcaster tucked into the former deputy's belt. *"Tiene!"* he shouted, pulling the trigger, causing a fireball to spew out of the weapon. The lawman burst into flames as Malcolm retrieved his gun.

The man screamed, flailing about as the fire consumed him. He panicked and ran away as he tried to put out the flames. Malcolm quickly cocked the hammer and turned it to the other interloper. *"Reothadh!"* he shouted, firing again. This time, when the bullet struck, a wave of frost enveloped his target, freezing him solid. Malcolm kicked the frozen statue, shattering it into a million pieces, then cocked the hammer of his weapon and aimed it at Dalton.

"Crith!" he said as he squeezed the trigger, sending a bullet at his enemy, but instead of hitting Dalton, it struck the dragonslayer, shattering the crystal embedded in the ricasso. Dalton didn't know what to do, so he quickly pulled it back

and plunged the sword into Alyssa from behind. She screamed as the blade ran her through, piercing her just below her sternum.

Malcolm looked at her as the rain pelted them—the tears of heaven crying down on them. It reminded him of the night she saved him from death and brought him into this world. When he looked in her eyes, as life slipped away from her, he saw nothing but love. The love they had shared these past few months, though fleeting, had given them both a renewed sense of hope for this world. Now, with this act of hatred, she was taken from him.

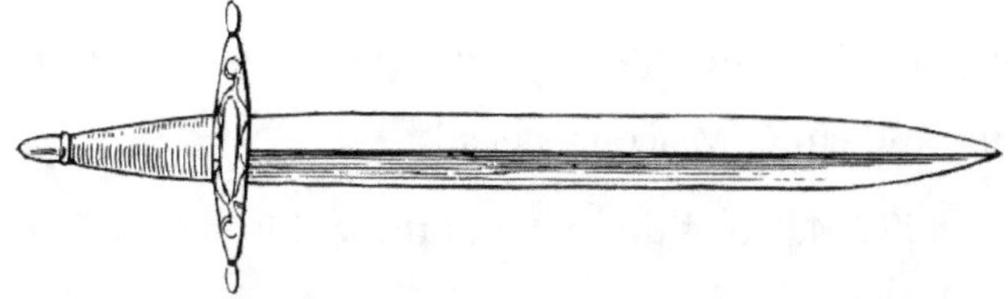

Dalton withdrew his sword as he pushed Alyssa to the ground. Malcolm knew he could kill him with one shot from his Spellcaster, but now it was personal. Malcolm tossed his handgun aside and picked up the sword of one of Dalton's fallen men. Although he wasn't a swordsman, Malcolm knew how to use one, and knew that he must do so to fight for the woman he loved.

Dalton sneered at Malcolm as they both assumed a high guard, circling each other. Their boots sank slightly in the mud as they tried to get their footing. Dalton threw an overhand cut, but Malcolm parried quickly, reflexively blocking his attack. Dalton tried again from the other side, but Malcolm eluded him again. They moved back and forth as Dalton kept throwing overhand cuts. Malcolm realized he could use this to his advantage.

With the next cut, Malcolm parried high, with his point towards Dalton's face. He nearly missed the moment to thrust, but attack he did, slapping the deputy's blade aside. Dalton did not fight the blow but turned the deflection into a swipe and cut at Malcolm's head.

Luckily, Malcolm dodged and thrust his blade at Dalton. He swerved to the side, but Malcolm's blade cut at his opponent's hand. Dalton stared in shock at two of his fingers, lying on the ground while the rest of his hand still held his sword.

Wasting no time gawking, Malcolm pressed on, sweeping his blade up to rest against Dalton's throat, expecting a surrender that didn't come—something grabbed Malcolm from behind, pinning his arms. It was the cohort that Malcolm had set on fire. The rain had doused the flames, leaving him badly burned but with enough strength to help his companion.

In that single moment, Dalton acted; he raised the dragonslayer overhead to strike Malcolm down. "It's over, Seger!" he boasted, reveling in his victory until he felt something cut him. Dalton lowered his sword hand to see it was gone—sliced clean off, as blood mixed with the rain and mud pooling on the open ground. Dalton screamed in pain as he gripped his bloody stump. He turned his head to see Alyssa standing behind him, alive and holding the Lord Marshal's sword.

As happy as Malcolm was to see Alyssa alive and well, he had to act quickly. He elbowed the man holding him, breaking free and thrusting the blade into him. He fell to the ground dead. Dalton continued to writhe in pain, clutching his bleeding stump close to his body. Malcolm threw down his sword and rushed over to Alyssa, holding her tight to ensure he wasn't dreaming. She dropped her sword and looked to her husband, clutching him tightly.

"You're alive! Thank God you're alive!" he cried as he kissed her face. "I thought I'd lost you!"

She just smiled and returned his tenderness. "You will never lose me, my love!" They held each other close, but their happiness was interrupted by Dalton's grimace.

"How? How are you alive? I stabbed you with the dragonslayer! You should be dead!"

"You have no knowledge of the anatomy of the Dragonkin," Alyssa said to him. "You missed my magical heart. I was able to heal my wounds and that of the Lord Marshal while you and Malcolm fought. You failed, Stalwart!"

"Besides, I rendered the sword useless with my Spellcaster," Malcolm interjected. "That's what the Lord Marshal whispered to me. He said if I could destroy the crystal in the sword, it would remove the dragonslayer's magic. Now, it's just an ordinary sword."

Dalton said nothing as all his schemes crumbled around him. He stumbled onto his feet and took off as fast as he could, rushing away from them. They both watched him run away like the coward he was.

"Will you let him go?" Alyssa asked. Malcolm said nothing—his anger still burned from everything Dalton had done to them and the Lord Marshal. He ran into the house and retrieved his Magi-Rifle, cocking back the hammer. He stared down the sight of this rifle at the fleeing coward, gauging the wind and rain as he took aim.

"*Bàs!*" he commanded, speaking the word for death as he pulled the trigger. The magic fueled the bullet as it shot out, a dark caliber of death that whistled through the air. Even in this storm, none could shake the resolve of a master magi-gunner as he struck his target. Dalton fell to the ground, dead before he even realized what had happened to him. His hatred and unwillingness to accept others killed him, as the magic within the bullet obliterated his soul.

Malcolm sat on the seat of his Land Cycle, adjusting the ether input controls as he prepared to take off into Fairhaven. He kept his Spellcaster holstered around his waist, but he also carried something new. Sheathed across from his weapon was the dragonslayer sword. It was still a good blade, sharp and sturdy, and it also acted as a reminder to Malcolm of his responsibility to protect the woman he loves.

A few months had passed since their encounter with Dalton Stalwart. The Lord Marshal survived his injuries, thanks to Alyssa's healing touch. For the sake of everyone involved, Sir Aleister decided to sweep the entire incident under the rug. Since Dalton and his compatriots were dismissed as deputies and left Fairhaven that morning, no one would report them missing.

Malcolm buried the bodies deep in the woods where no one would find them, a fitting end for these troublemakers. During the Endless War, many of the dead were buried in unmarked graves. They would just be counted amongst the millions lost in 300 years of fighting if they were ever discovered.

Even still, Malcolm didn't feel right about it. He wanted Dalton's crimes laid out for all to see, but that would expose the Lord Marshal, the refugee villagers of Sgothan Heights, and even Alyssa. It was better this way, but Malcolm hated covering up their crimes. He thought a public recitation would expose their malignancy and help change people's attitudes toward the Dragonkin.

In the end, they would just have to continue down the road they were on—both he and Alyssa—to make people understand the place Dragonkin had within human society. For them, that road led to bringing in a new life into the world.

Malcolm turned his head as the door to the house creaked open. Mrs. Tomlin walked out, followed by Alyssa holding onto her slightly pronounced belly. For being only four months pregnant, she carried herself quite well. Malcolm was told it was because Dragonkin babies had tails and wings, making them more prominent in the womb. Even a half-human/half-Dragonkin baby like theirs would share these characteristics, so they ensured Lily stopped by for regular visits.

"How are they doing, Lily? He seems to be kicking up a storm as of late," Malcolm said, garnering the ire of Alyssa with the assumption that their child was a boy.

"She is doing just fine," Alyssa snapped back at him, "full of fire, just like her mother."

"Now, now, there'll be no more of that, you two," Lily scolded them. "It doesn't matter if it's a boy or a girl as long the child has a loving home. You should be more worried about picking names than arguing about the child's sex."

"Oh, we already decided on that," Malcolm interjected. "If it's a boy, Henry, after my father."

"And if it's a girl, Serene, after my grandmother," Alyssa added. "It's the one thing we could agree on completely. Now, if only someone would finish the nursery before the baby is born . . ."

"Lyssa, I can't rush it. The foundation of this house is older than I am. I don't want to build a nursery only to have it collapse on him, or her, shortly after the baby's born."

Alyssa frowned at the excuses Malcolm was making, but she knew his concerns were justified. Luckily, Lily had a solution. "You know, my brother and his family will be visiting next week. He built his own home in Hawksmoor. He might be able to give you some help and advice on building your new addition."

"Oh no, Lily, I wouldn't want to impose on your brother while he's visiting you," Alyssa said.

"Nonsense Alyssa dear, I insist. Besides, if I don't give the lazy slob something to do, he'll just spend his entire visit fishing with Tony, leaving me to run the clinic by myself."

Lily handed Malcolm a basket of medicine and fresh supplies for the clinic from Alyssa. He took them and gave her a pair of goggles for the ride back to Fairhaven. Once the basket was snug in the compartment under the seat, he grabbed his leather coat off the railing on the front porch.

"Will you be back soon? You're making me dinner tonight, remember?" Alyssa reminded him. "It's meatloaf night, you promised!"

Lily looked confused at the two. "Meat-loaf?" she exclaimed, enunciating each word. "What in God's name is meat-loaf?"

"An old family recipe, Mrs. Tomlin. Alyssa didn't like the idea at first, but being pregnant, it's what she's craving right now, "he explained before turning back to Alyssa and putting his coat on. "I should only be gone about an hour, maybe two. Sir Aleister asked me to visit the Jericho place. They keep damming up the creek running through their land, preventing the water from flowing to the McAllister farm.

We've warned them to stop doing it, so this time, it may take a little more persuasion."

"The Lord Marshal's new enforcer at it again, eh?" she replied, patting the new emblem on his coat. It was the coat of arms of Fawleen, designating Malcolm as a deputy marshal. Sir Aleister hadn't hesitated to ask him to fill the open position. He wanted someone he could trust, and Malcolm was the most trustworthy man in the parish.

"It helps pay for that new addition I'm building. Besides, once a magi-gunner, always a magi-gunner," Malcolm said as he kissed her goodbye. He loved her more than life itself; something they had proven to each other all those months ago. Now they could start on their path of building a family.

"Oh, that reminds me!" Malcolm recalled as he rushed over to the Land Cycle and pulled out something from the inner compartment. He strolled back toward Alyssa and presented her with a gift, simply wrapped in brown paper.

"What's this?" she asked. Malcolm didn't say anything. He simply motioned for her to open it. She peeled back the paper to reveal a new leather-bound writing journal, her eyes lighting with excitement.

"Your old journal was from the war. This one is for the new life—the new family—we're starting here in Fairhaven," he explained. Alyssa loved the idea and kissed him again, hugging him tight around the neck.

"Thank you, Mal! I love it!"

"I expect you'll have some new poems to read to our baby!" he said with one last kiss before he got on the Land Cycle. Once Lily was on, they both waved to Alyssa as they drove off. Alyssa stood there, watching them until they rode out of view.

Alyssa walked up on the front porch and sat on the swing that Malcolm had built. She swayed slowly back and forth as she opened the book and pulled out a pencil from her apron. Her back arched as she reached around, trying to relieve the pressure and the pain. She could not wait for the baby to be born, but she would find solace in her poetry until then. It would be something she could share with her child; to tell them what their parents had sacrificed and endured to bring them into this world. And how two strangers fell in love across the River of Souls.

Her belly became a warzone.

Skin stretched,

headaches hurt,

baby bounced

and spun inside her womb.

She felt all the pains that come with

bringing new life into this world.

Her body was creating a creature

mixed from two beings.

Child of Love, your mother's instinct

was so in tune she was considered a shieldmaiden.

Child of Love, your father's swordsmanship

was so respected that others dare not do you wrong.

It was a fight to get you here with us,

but remember, sweet one,

you are a child born from love.

Mark Piggott, a native of Phillipsburg, New Jersey, enlisted in the U.S. Navy in 1982, beginning a 23-year career. He served on four aircraft carriers and various duty stations as a Navy Journalist before he attained the rank of Chief Petty Officer. He retired from active duty in 2006. Mark currently works as a writer-editor for the Department of Housing and Urban Development. He and his wife, Georgiene, reside in Alexandria, Virginia. They have three children.

To find out more about his award-winning fantasy and steampunk novels, visit authormarkpiggott.com.